FROM THE
NANCY DREW FILES

THE CASE: Nancy investigates a case of diamonds, deception, and death.

CONTACT: The evidence points to jewelry designer Marcia Cheung, who needs Nancy's help to clear her name.

SUSPECTS: Cy Baxter—the rival jeweler accuses Marcia of stealing the gems but may have pocketed them himself.

Len Olson—Marcia's fiancé is trying to start his own business, and he may have found the ideal get-rich-quick scheme.

Morgan Fowler—the Carmel security guard has dreams of a career in Hollywood, and a fistful of diamonds could open a lot of doors.

COMPLICATIONS: Nancy knows that her only chance to find the real killer is to locate the real diamonds . . . and the only person with a clue is Joanna Burton—the victim.

Books in The Nancy Drew Files® Series

Available from ARCHWAY Paperbacks

Case 83
Diamond Deceit
Carolyn Keene

AN ARCHWAY PAPERBACK
Published by POCKET BOOKS

New York   London   Toronto   Sydney   Tokyo   Singapore

AN ARCHWAY PAPERBACK *Original*

An Archway Paperback published by
POCKET BOOKS, a division of Simon & Schuster Inc.
1230 Avenue of the Americas, New York, NY 10020

Copyright © 1993 by Simon & Schuster Inc.
Produced by Mega-Books of New York, Inc.

ISBN: 0-671-73087-8

First Archway Paperback printing May 1993

10 9 8 7 6 5 4 3 2 1

NANCY DREW, AN ARCHWAY PAPERBACK and colophon are registered trademarks of Simon & Schuster Inc.

THE NANCY DREW FILES is a trademark of Simon & Schuster Inc.

Cover art by Tricia Zimic

Printed in the U.S.A.

IL 6+

Diamond Deceit

Chapter

One

I *HATE* SITTING around, waiting for the phone to ring," George Fayne said, glaring at the telephone on Nancy Drew's bedside table.

"You hate sitting around, period," Nancy said with a laugh. "Maybe when Bess told Hannah she was going to call at three o'clock she meant *California* time. They're two hours behind us."

George checked her watch again. "If she doesn't call soon, we're going to lose our court time." She picked up her tennis racket and started practicing a restrained forehand in the middle of the room.

Nancy glanced at herself in the mirror—her tennis dress was blindingly white. "I wonder what's kept Bess in California," she said, tying her reddish blond hair back. "Her mom and dad came back over a week ago."

1

Bess Marvin, who was George's cousin and Nancy's good friend, had gone to Carmel, California, to visit friends of her parents.

"My aunt was pretty vague about why Bess decided to stay," George said, flopping down on Nancy's bed. She shot Nancy a teasing glance. "Maybe you'd better investigate, Nan."

"I don't need a new mystery," Nancy said, shaking her head. At eighteen Nancy had a reputation as an excellent detective.

In spite of George's grumbling, Nancy knew George missed Bess. It was amazing to Nancy that two people as different as Bess and George could be so inseparable. George had short, dark hair and the long, lean body of an athlete. Bess, on the other hand, was petite, curvy, and blond. The only sports she participated in were dating and marathon shopping.

The phone rang, and George didn't hesitate to grab the receiver. "Hello? Bess! You were supposed to call over an hour ago. Nancy and I are going to miss our tennis match."

George motioned for Nancy to put her ear close so they could both hear what Bess was saying.

"Sorry, but I got tied up," Bess said without any further explanation.

George rolled her eyes. With Bess that probably meant she'd met some cute guy and lost track of the time.

"So what gives?" Nancy said into the receiver. "Why did you extend your vacation?"

"You guys, I really love it out here." Nancy could hear the enthusiasm in Bess's voice even over the phone.

"Then there must be lots of good shopping, good food, and great-looking guys," George teased.

"I'm serious," Bess said. "I think you'd like it, too. In fact . . ." She hesitated a moment, then said in a rush, "I was wondering if maybe you'd come out to see how great Carmel is. There'd be plenty of golf and tennis for you, George. I also found some shops that I know you guys will love. And you can stay with me at the Provence Inn. Mr. and Mrs. Menendez, my parents' friends, run it."

Nancy had to admit that Carmel sounded great. Still, Nancy had the feeling that Bess was holding something back. "Is everything okay there?" she asked.

"It's all great!" Bess replied. "We'd really have a super time—I'd love you to come." There was a long pause before Bess added, "And I have one teeny surprise for you."

"What's that?" George asked suspiciously.

"You have to come here to find out," Bess said mysteriously.

Nancy could hear her say something to someone else, but she couldn't make out the words.

Putting her hand over the mouthpiece, Nancy spoke to George. "Why don't we go? Dad is tied up with a trial now, and Ned is working hard at school." Ned Nickerson was Nancy's longtime boyfriend and a student at Emerson College.

George nodded once slowly, then more eagerly. "Sounds good to me."

Nancy removed her hand and spoke into the receiver. "Okay, we'll come. We'll call you back tonight and let you know when our flight arrives."

"I can't wait to see you! I can't wait for you to meet Ted!" The phone clicked, and the line went dead.

"Ted," George repeated, grinning at Nancy. "So *that's* what this is all about."

"I can't believe Bess isn't here to meet us," George said. She dropped her suitcase and golf clubs in the middle of the room she and Nancy were sharing at the Provence Inn.

"Mrs. Menendez said there was some sort of problem at her son's restaurant." Nancy paused, then added, "Still, I'm not sure why that would keep *Bess* from meeting us."

The two girls were surprised that Bess hadn't met them at the airport as they'd arranged. She merely left a message that she'd been delayed.

"We'll have to wait until she shows up and explains," George said with a shrug.

"If Bess had picked us up, we wouldn't have

4

rented a car. Now we can come and go as we please."

While Nancy unpacked she checked out the room Mrs. Menendez had given her and George. It was cheerful and bright, with white plaster walls, a white brick fireplace outlined with navy and white tiles, and blue-and-white-patterned bedspreads and curtains.

"If it stays this chilly, we'll need to use the fireplace," George said, zipping up the jacket of her navy and red running suit.

"Bess warned me the weather in Carmel can be cool." Nancy was glad she'd packed a heavy turquoise sweater to wear with her black jeans.

Nancy went to the window and peered out at the central courtyard, which the Menendezes had planted with bright and colorful flowers. The inn was just up the road from the beach, and Nancy opened the window a crack to smell the salty sea air.

"I'm starved," George announced. Nancy turned around to see her friend opening cabinets and the refrigerator in the small kitchenette on the opposite side of their room.

"Mrs. Menendez said that her son Ted's restaurant is just up the hill. Why don't we walk up there, get something to eat, and surprise Bess?" Nancy suggested.

"Good idea," George agreed. "Besides, I want to find out what's going on with Bess and this Ted guy."

"The restaurant is on Ocean Avenue, the same street we're on," Nancy said. "Ocean goes down to the beach, but the restaurant is the other way, back *up* this hill. It's called the Café de Carmel."

Outside the inn, Nancy and George looked down toward the ocean. Ocean Avenue was lined with little shops and houses, all different from one another. There were stucco houses with red tiled roofs and cute little wooden cottages with picket fences.

"Bess is right about this place. It's absolutely gorgeous," Nancy said, grinning.

"Listen to those waves," George said. "I wonder if there's any surfing."

"We'll have plenty of time for the beach once we hook up with Bess," Nancy said. "We're going to be here until Tuesday, and it's only Thursday."

Nancy and George started up the steep hill to the restaurant. They walked slowly, peering into one shop window after another. One shop had nothing but scarves, hats, and other accessories. Another sold only kites in wild shapes and colors.

"Mrs. Menendez wasn't kidding when she said up the hill," George commented.

"It *is* steep," Nancy agreed, "but there's so much to look at I don't mind."

In the middle of the second block George stopped at the window of a jewelry shop. The words Cheung Original Designs were painted in gold letters in a small circle in a corner of the window.

"Those are just what I've been looking for," George said, pointing at a pair of gold geometric earrings.

"I thought you were starved," Nancy said.

"Everything can wait for new jewelry," George answered back, winking.

The girls were startled just then by the sound of angry voices from inside the shop. Peering through the glass door, Nancy saw a tall, blond young man shaking his finger at a shorter, stocky, balding man. When the blond man grabbed the older man's shirt, the older man pulled away.

"What's this all about?" Nancy wondered aloud.

Before she knew what was happening, the door to the shop burst open. Nancy was caught in the path of the balding man, who shoved her back against a wall. The young man followed close behind, an angry expression marring his good looks. Neither man seemed to notice Nancy at all.

The balding man paused at the edge of the curb before turning around to face the younger man. Nancy detected a trace of challenge in his expression as he opened his mouth to speak.

"Save it, Baxter," the blond man snapped, cutting off the older man's words. The young man took a threatening step toward Baxter, his face red and his fists clenched at his sides. "If one word of this gets out, you're as good as dead!"

7

Chapter

Two

N ANCY WAS taken aback at the venom in the young man's words. Glancing over at George, Nancy saw that her friend appeared to be too shocked to move or say anything.

Baxter turned his back on the other man, jerked open the door of a black Jaguar parked at the curb, and climbed into the driver's seat. He stared pointedly at the younger man as he locked the doors.

"Baxter, you can't just drive off," the young man shouted. He pounded on the hood of the Jaguar with his balled-up fists, his face red with rage.

Baxter lowered his car window and spoke for the first time. "Keep your filthy hands off my car," he snapped, then he pulled away from the curb.

The younger man stood glaring at the car until it disappeared around a corner. Finally he went back into the small shop.

As he brushed by Nancy again she noticed dirt and grass stains on his faded blue jeans and white T-shirt. His long blond hair was bleached almost white from the sun, and his skin was deeply tanned.

Nancy watched him go behind a display case and put his arm around a petite woman dressed in a long embroidered tunic and silk slacks. She had a single thick black braid and dark, almond-shaped eyes. A third person in the shop, an older woman, was dressed in black slacks and a blue blazer and was talking seriously to the couple.

"What was *that* all about?" George asked, joining Nancy. "Those guys practically knocked you down!"

"I'm fine," Nancy assured her. "But I wonder—"

"Nancy! George! I can't believe you're finally here!"

Nancy turned to see Bess running across Ocean Avenue toward her and George. She was wearing a white blouse and a black jeans skirt, covered by a red apron with Café de Carmel printed on it in white. Bess gave both girls a big hug.

Nancy noticed that a stocky young man in his early twenties had followed Bess across the street. He had straight dark hair and was wearing black jeans and a white button-down shirt. Standing on the curb a few feet from the girls, he crossed his arms over his chest.

"Come over here." Bess took the young man by the arm and pulled him into their circle. "This is Ted Menendez," she told Nancy and George, grinning from ear to ear.

Ted shook hands briefly with both girls. He smiled, showing even, white teeth. "I'm glad you were able to come visit," he said. "Bess has told me a lot about you two."

Despite his warm words, Nancy noticed that Ted's eyes never made contact with hers. His handshake was too quick, almost mechanical. Maybe he was just nervous, she reasoned.

"How do you like your room at the inn?" Bess asked, keeping her arm linked with Ted's.

Nancy let George answer. Her own attention was distracted as the older woman came out of the jewelry shop and detoured around Nancy's group.

"Earth to Nancy," Bess's voice broke into Nancy's thoughts a moment later.

"Oh—sorry, Bess," Nancy said. "I got caught up thinking about something that just happened here."

"Nancy was almost trampled by two men who ran out of that shop a couple of minutes ago. One of them was shouting threats at the other one," George explained.

"You mean Len?" Ted asked worriedly. "A big

blond guy?" Nancy and George nodded. "I hope it's nothing serious. I'm going to see what happened here. Bess, can you cover for me at the restaurant?" He squeezed her hand.

Bess shook her head and smiled up at Ted. From the way they looked at each other, Nancy guessed that George was right. Ted probably *was* the reason Bess had extended her vacation.

"Len's a good friend of mine," Ted explained to Nancy and George. "We've gotten to know each other pretty well coaching Little League baseball." With that he entered the jewelry shop.

"I hope everything's okay," George said to Bess. "But right now I just remembered I'm starving! It's a good thing Ted owns a restaurant."

"Actually, it belongs to his parents. Ted just runs it for them," Bess explained.

"He sure is cute. No wonder you decided to stay a little longer," Nancy said, raising an eyebrow at her friend.

"Ted's nice," Bess said, blushing slightly. "But he's not the only reason I decided to stay."

"Bess, can we talk about this over some food?" George asked.

Bess laughed and linked her arm through George's. "Sure. Come on over to the restaurant, and I'll feed you."

Bess led them across the street and through a doorway with a sign that read Café de Carmel.

Nancy paused just inside the door to check out

the place. The lower half of each wall was covered in black and white tile. Neon-filled tubes shaped like musical instruments were placed on the upper wall space. Chrome-edged tables and red vinyl chairs filled the room. A jukebox stood against one wall. Even though it was the middle of the afternoon, several tables were filled.

Bess pointed to a table near the jukebox. "You two sit down, and I'll get you something to eat," she said. "I'm just going to bring you something light. We're having a big picnic dinner on the beach with Ted's parents later," she added, disappearing through a red swinging door at the rear of the café.

"I guess this isn't the first time Bess has helped Ted out," George said to Nancy as they sat down. "She seems to know her way around here."

Just then the restaurant door opened, and Ted entered, followed by the tall blond guy from the jewelry shop. They came over and joined Nancy and George.

"This is Len Olson," Ted said. "He and his fiancée, Marcia Cheung, rent the shop across the street. Len's a landscape architect, and Marcia's a jewelry designer. Bess told me you're a detective, Nancy, and I was wondering if you'd listen to what Len has to say."

Bess came out of the kitchen with two bowls of steaming soup, which she set in front of Nancy and George. "I'll get you one, too, Len," she offered.

"That's okay. Why don't you sit down while I tell your friend what happened to Marcia?" Len said.

Bess stared first at Ted and then at Len. Then she shook a reproving finger in their faces. "Oh, no, you don't! Nancy's here on vacation, not to solve any mysteries."

"I don't mind," Nancy said. "Really."

Bess pulled up a chair from a neighboring table and placed it between Nancy and Ted. While she settled in, Len picked up a napkin from the table and started folding it into smaller and smaller squares. Nancy sensed his tension. He seemed ready to explode.

"Why don't you tell me who that man was you were yelling at, Len?" she prompted.

Crumpling the napkin, Len threw it down. "That was Cy Baxter," he said angrily.

"Cy's another jewelry designer who has a shop here in Carmel," Ted explained. "He's pretty well known."

"Marcia worked for Cy until about six months ago, when we could finally afford to rent our own place," Len added. "Marcia has a studio in the back of the shop where she designs and makes the jewelry she sells. I run my landscaping business out of the same office. All I really need are some filing cabinets and a phone. I keep my equipment on my truck. Anyway, Marcia just finished designing a new setting for some diamonds that belong to Joanna Burton."

13

"Joanna Burton! The movie star?" Bess interrupted, her mouth falling open.

"Yup," Len said. "I don't think she's made a movie for years, though. Anyway, Miss Burton lives here in Carmel," he went on. "We thought that designing a necklace for a movie star would help Marcia build her reputation." Len shook his head. "We never dreamed something like this would happen."

"Something like what?" Nancy questioned.

"Did you notice an older woman in the shop?" Nancy and George both nodded. "She's a police detective. Joanna Burton filed a report claiming that the diamonds in her necklace had been replaced with fakes."

"Oh, no!" George said, swallowing a spoonful of soup. "Did she accuse Marcia?"

Len shook his head. "No, she was just asking general questions. But while she was there Cy Baxter came in. He was the one who accused Marcia. He said that she probably switched the stones and kept the diamonds for herself."

"How did he know that the diamonds had been switched?" Nancy wanted to know.

"Joanna Burton had given him the necklace to appraise. That was when he discovered that the diamonds in it were really cubic zirconia." Seeing the confused looks on the girls' faces, he explained, "Cubic zirconia is a stone that resembles diamonds. It's often used in jewelry imitations. To the untrained eye, c.z. looks like the real thing. I know *I* can't tell the difference."

Len sat silently for a few moments, his face a deep red. He was obviously very upset by what had happened. Nancy decided to give him a chance to get himself under control, so she took a few spoonfuls of her soup. It was a delicious, light vegetable puree.

Without warning Len banged his fist on the tabletop, startling Nancy. "He had no right!" Len burst out angrily. "Who does Baxter think he is, walking in and making a statement like that? Marcia would never replace real stones with fakes and then try to keep the diamonds!"

Nancy felt uneasy. There was something scary about Len's explosive temper.

Len fell silent again for a minute before turning to Nancy. "Do you think you could try to find out what really happened to the diamonds?" he asked. "Marcia didn't do it, I swear." Len banged his fist down again, causing the bowls of soup to clatter on the tabletop. "If this gets out, no one will let Marcia touch any jewelry. It could ruin her business!"

Len must have noticed how uncomfortable Nancy was with his anger because he slowly leaned back in his chair, rubbing his temples. "Look, I'm sorry. I guess I got a little carried away. Please help us," he said in a softer voice.

Nancy wasn't sure she wanted to get involved

with this case. She was uneasy with Len's temper, and she *was* on vacation, but his story had definitely aroused her curiosity.

Finally she turned to Len and said, "I'll need to talk to Marcia."

"Great," Len told her. "Can she meet with you this evening after she closes the shop? Around eight?"

Bess said in an excited whisper, "Hey, maybe we should go talk to Joanna Burton, too. Do you know where she lives, Len?"

"She lives in one of the big houses along Seventeen-Mile Drive," Ted answered for Len. "It's a coast road lined with golf courses and fancy homes. Lots of movie people live there. They even charge a toll to drive along the road to look."

"Marcia has her phone number, if you want to make an appointment to see her," Len added.

Nancy's mind raced ahead. "What about Cy Baxter?" she asked. "How far is it to his store? I'd like to find out a little more about his part in all this."

"I'll go along and show you," Bess said.

"Bess?" Ted looked at her critically. "You're leaving? Now?"

Bess was surprised by Ted's response. "We won't take long. We'll be back," she assured him.

"But it's getting close to the time for our picnic," Ted said. "Do you really think you should go?"

Nancy didn't understand Ted's reaction. Bess had invited her and George to Carmel. Surely he knew that Bess would be spending time with them. Why was he being so possessive?

Len didn't appear to notice the tension that had settled over the group. "Then you'll try to find out what happened?" he asked Nancy.

"I'm not making any promises, but it can't hurt to ask a few questions," Nancy replied.

"Thanks," Len said. He took Nancy's hand and shook it. "I really appreciate it." He stood up and headed toward the door. "I'm going to tell Marcia right now."

Nancy, Bess, and George also got up. " 'Bye, Ted. See you in a little while," George said.

Ted folded his arms and stared at Nancy and George as they walked past him. Nancy shivered. The cold anger in Ted's dark eyes chilled her.

Chapter

Three

WHAT'S WITH that guy?" George whispered to Nancy as soon as they got outside. Nancy could tell that George had also picked up on Ted's anger.

Nancy shrugged. "Isn't Bess coming?" she asked, noticing that their friend hadn't left with them.

George pointed into the restaurant. "It looks as if there's trouble in paradise. I don't think Ted wants Bess to go with us."

Ted and Bess were standing right inside the café, talking. Bess's face was flushed, and she seemed to be close to tears. Ted was holding both of her arms and was speaking very seriously.

Ted glanced up and met Nancy's gaze. His expression immediately changed. After saying something more to Bess, he smiled down at her and kissed her on the cheek. A moment later Bess had joined Nancy and George on the sidewalk.

"What was that all about?" George asked her cousin as soon as the door closed.

"He's just worried that I'll get into trouble with you guys," Bess said, not very convincingly. "I never should have told him some of the things that had happened to us on cases with Nancy."

Nancy hated to see her friend torn between Ted and them. "You don't have to come with us if you don't want to," Nancy said to Bess. "Just point us in the right direction."

"There's no way I'm going to miss this," Bess said firmly. "I *want* to go. Besides, Ted needs to learn to let go a little. He's been spoiled having me all to himself," she added, giggling.

"So what's the story with you two, anyway?" George asked. "Is this a major romance?" Nancy could tell that George hoped it wasn't.

Bess shrugged. "I don't know. Not too major, I guess. But Ted's really nice," Bess added with a grin.

She led the way up the hill to the next corner, then turned left. While they walked Nancy went over all that Len had told them about the diamond necklace.

"Have you had a chance to get to know Marcia at all?" Nancy asked Bess.

"I only met her briefly when she and Len ate at

the restaurant," Bess answered. "She seems nice."

Nancy was anxious to meet the designer and form her own impressions. She couldn't know for sure that Marcia *hadn't* switched the diamonds until she investigated.

When the girls were halfway down the block, Bess stopped in front of a shop a little larger than Cheung Original Designs. A small sign over the door identified the store as Baxter's Fine Jewelry. "Here it is," Bess announced, opening the door.

A bell chimed when Nancy, Bess, and George stepped into the shop. Nancy immediately spotted the short, balding man who had stormed out of Marcia's store earlier. He was standing behind the jewelry counter, scolding a woman in her forties who was apparently one of his employees. She was wearing a plain black dress, and her long, dark hair was streaked with gray.

"I've asked you over and over to use this when removing a stone from its setting, not this." Baxter held up a small instrument to illustrate his point. "And never leave a customer out here in the showroom alone. Can't I leave you in the shop for even ten minutes without you screwing up?"

The woman made no attempt to defend herself. She simply stared at the floor as Baxter went on and on. Nancy was embarrassed to be there. She stared at a Seaside Security sticker in the corner of the window, trying to pretend she wasn't there. If this was the way Cy Baxter treated his employees, she thought, Marcia must have been happy to branch out on her own.

Bess and George seemed to be as embarrassed as Nancy to be witnessing the argument. After standing there uneasily for a moment Bess pulled Nancy and George over to a display of gold charms for bracelets. "Aren't these darling?" she asked.

Cy Baxter broke off abruptly as if he had just realized the girls were there. "We'll be with you in a moment," he said politely. Turning back to his assistant, he lowered his voice so Nancy couldn't hear what he was saying.

"I think Mr. Baxter makes these himself," Bess went on. "This is the lone cypress—that's a tree that grows along the Seventeen-Mile Drive. And these are sea otters. I want to make sure you see some real ones while you're—"

Just then the showroom erupted in noise as dozens of clocks lining one wall of the store began to chime the hour.

"Look at that cuckoo clock," George said, pointing at a carved wooden clock whose painted wooden bird popped out to announce the time. "It's pretty cute."

"That one also performs on the quarter hour," Cy Baxter said. He had come out from behind the counter to join them. His assistant was just disappearing into a room at the rear of the store. "Would you like me to take it down so you can look at it close up?"

"No, thank you, anyway," Nancy said.

"Can I show you anything else? A necklace? Rings?" Baxter inquired. He was checking the girls over carefully as he talked.

Nancy hesitated, trying to decide what approach would work best with the store owner. "Um, my name is Nancy Drew," she said, stalling.

Baxter peeked at his watch. Nancy decided right then that he wouldn't give any of his time to anyone but a customer. She'd just have to ask the right questions and hope he liked to talk. "I'm looking for someone to design a bracelet," she went on. "I've talked to several people around Carmel asking for recommendations. Your name came up." Nancy paused before adding, "So did Marcia Cheung's."

"Marcia used to work for me," Baxter said curtly. "Not that she ever appreciated all the things I taught her."

He was obviously bitter about Marcia's departure, Nancy thought. "I understand that she recently designed a necklace for Joanna Burton," she said.

Baxter's face darkened for just an instant. Then he cleared his throat and said, "Miss Burton is a customer of mine, also."

"Oh, really? Why did she ask Marcia to do her necklace?"

Nancy expected the store owner to become angry, but instead he leaned conspiratorially toward the girls. "I've done a lot of work for Miss Burton in the past, but now—how should I put this?—she doesn't always pay her bills. She asked me to design a new setting for her necklace, but at the time she owed me for some work I'd done months earlier, so I refused. Now I wish I had done the design."

"If Miss Burton doesn't always pay, why do you wish you'd designed the necklace?" Bess asked curiously.

Way to go, Bess! Nancy silently applauded her friend. She hoped Bess's comment would get Baxter talking about the fake stones.

"It's not general knowledge yet," Baxter began, then he hesitated. He finally continued, "When Joanna got the necklace back her diamonds were gone, replaced with c.z.—that's cubic zirconia."

Cy Baxter took a deep breath, clapping his hands together. "Well, enough of that. What kind of bracelet were you considering? Perhaps we'd better talk—"

"But what happened to the diamonds?" George pressed, leaning over the counter.

"I can't say, but that necklace wasn't anywhere but Marcia Cheung's shop," he said, stressing her name.

Nancy still had one more question to ask. "How did you know the diamonds were replaced?"

"I saw them. Joanna needed to have the new setting appraised for her insurance, and I do appraisals for insurance companies," Baxter explained. "When I was examining the necklace, I noticed that the gold prongs holding the stones were scratched. That didn't look like Marcia's usual work—after all, I had trained her. So I took a closer look."

"How could you tell the stones were fakes?" George asked.

"Cubic zirconia weighs more than diamonds," the jeweler informed the girls. "After almost thirty years in the business I can definitely tell a fake when I see one."

Nancy nodded, then changed the subject. "About how long does it take to have jewelry appraised? I have some pieces—"

Cy Baxter smiled and said, "Just bring them in anytime. I can usually examine the piece and write up a report within twenty-four hours."

"So Nancy would have to leave her jewelry here?" Bess inquired. Nancy knew right away what her friend was getting at. Joanna Burton must have left her necklace with Cy Baxter, too. That meant Cy himself would have had the chance to replace the diamonds.

"Of course. But it would be perfectly safe,"

Baxter assured her. "Now, what kind of bracelet did you want designed, Miss Drew?"

"I really haven't any ideas," Nancy replied.

She, Bess, and George patiently waited while Cy Baxter showed them examples of his work. His pieces were very traditional, different from Marcia's more modern ones.

Saying she was unable to make up her mind, Nancy politely thanked the jeweler and signed his guest register. Just as they were leaving, the painted bird popped out of the cuckoo clock and performed its solo. It was a quarter past six.

As they started back to the Café de Carmel, Nancy turned to her friends and said, "Did you guys hear what Baxter said? It takes him twenty-four hours to appraise something. Joanna Burton probably had to leave her necklace overnight."

"He could have stolen the diamonds during that time," Bess added.

"But why would he switch Joanna Burton's stones and then tell her about it?" George wanted to know.

Nancy shrugged. "Maybe because he knew he could blame it on someone else. Baxter didn't seem to be happy that Marcia left him to open her own jewelry store. Maybe he decided to steal the diamonds and ruin Marcia's reputation at the same time."

With a frown she added, "Something else he told us doesn't make sense. Baxter said that there were scratches on the prongs that held the fake stones in place. I don't think an experienced jeweler like Marcia Cheung would leave scratches, do you?"

"I've heard only good things about Marcia's work," Bess said. "Ted's going to be wondering what happened to us," she added with a nervous laugh as they approached Café de Carmel. "It's almost six-thirty. That's the time we're supposed to meet his parents on the beach."

George said excitedly, "I can't wait to see the ocean."

Bess pushed open the restaurant door, and a waitress instantly appeared. "Hi, Libby," Bess greeted the red-haired girl. "Just stopped by to pick up Ted."

"Ted went on ahead. He was kind of mad," Libby said. "He said to tell you he meant six-thirty Pacific time, not Central time."

Bess's eyebrows drew together in a worried frown. Then she turned to Nancy and George and laughed. "I guess we'd better get down there before they eat everything." She herded Nancy and George out the door, then set a brisk pace for their walk to the beach.

"Hey, slow down," George said. "I've never known you to go so fast."

"We'll only be about five minutes late. That's

not such a big deal," Nancy added. Bess seemed to be awfully concerned about disappointing Ted. Nancy was beginning to think that maybe Ted's expectations were a little unreasonable.

When they reached the beach, Bess turned left and walked along the road.

"Oh, this is beautiful!" George exclaimed, pausing.

Nancy had to agree. A steep, sandy hill descended some twenty feet to the beach below. Several wooden stairways led down to the flat sand. Out on the water the sun's glow seemed to color the entire Pacific Ocean.

"Mmm," Bess said distractedly. "Ted said he'd build the fire down the beach this way, by one of the staircases." She scanned, then pointed. "There they are! See the fire?"

Nancy and George followed as Bess hurried to the first staircase and took the steps to the beach. "She seems awfully nervous," George commented. "What's the big deal?"

Ted was about fifty feet away with two other people. A fire blazed beside them, and a blanket had been spread out on the beach near it.

Nancy recognized Mrs. Menendez, of course. The heavyset woman with short dark hair had checked Nancy and George into their room. The other man had the same dark hair and stocky build as Ted. He had to be Mr. Menendez, Nancy guessed.

"I guess you met Mrs. Menendez at the inn earlier," Bess told Nancy and George. "This is Ted's dad. You can see where Ted gets his good looks," Bess said.

Mr. Menendez acted embarrassed, but Nancy could tell he loved Bess's compliment. "It's nice to meet you girls. I hope you like it here in Carmel," he said. Then he sat with his wife.

"So far we love it," George assured him.

Ted continued to stare out at the water, Nancy noticed. He made no move to greet her or George. Was he still mad that they had taken Bess to Cy Baxter's shop? Nancy stifled the irritation that rose inside her. She wanted to give Bess's new boyfriend a chance, after all.

Bess acted as if she were bursting with a secret. Tapping Ted on the shoulder, she whispered something into his ear and got him to turn around.

"Hey, cuz," George said. "You convinced Nancy and me to travel all this way because you said you had a surprise for us. We've been here almost half a day, and we still haven't been surprised. What gives?"

Bess's blue eyes were sparkling. "Maybe you'd better sit down," she said to George and Nancy, indicating the blanket.

"This must be big," Nancy said, plopping down next to George.

Bess grabbed Ted's arm, and Nancy exchanged an uneasy look with George. She had a feeling that this was going to be really big. Was Bess thinking of getting married?

Bess took a deep breath and let it out. She focused first on George, then on Nancy, and said, "You guys, I'm thinking about moving to Carmel!"

Chapter

Four

Nancy was so shocked that all she could do was stare at Bess. Bess move away from River Heights? Nancy couldn't imagine it. Maybe she hadn't heard correctly. One look at her friend's face, though, and Nancy knew that Bess was serious.

Nancy saw the same stunned expression that she knew that she herself must be wearing on George's face. Suddenly George smiled at Bess and said, "Okay, really now. What's the surprise?"

"That *is* the surprise," Bess said, acting less sure of herself.

George faced her cousin. "But, Bess, do you really want to move away from River Heights? I mean, what are you going to do here?"

For the first time Nancy glanced at Ted. He was beaming. Nancy felt a little jealous that Bess would choose Ted over her and George. She wanted to be happy for Bess, but instead she just felt a little—hurt. How could Bess make a decision like this without even consulting her and George?

"I haven't told you everything yet," Bess said. "The very first day my parents and I got here, the pastry chef at Café de Carmel quit. I mentioned that I'd learned how to make desserts at the Claude DuPres International Cooking School. Ted asked me to help out, and everybody loved my fruit tarts," Bess said proudly.

"The next day I made split lemon cake," Bess went on. "I guess word spread, because people came in all afternoon asking for it."

Ted reached over to give Bess's shoulders a squeeze. "Our Desserts by Bess have become the in thing," he added.

"We're very proud of Bess," Mrs. Menendez said, giving Bess a warm smile. "We've always had a good business on the weekends with tourists, but now we seem to be busy all the time."

"And it's all because of those fattening desserts Bess does so well." Mr. Menendez patted his stomach.

"That's why I couldn't pick you up at the airport," Bess told Nancy and George. "I had a rush order for napoleons, and I had to make sure they were ready. I knew you'd understand. You guys know I'm going to miss you, but this is an opportunity for me to do something on my own."

Bess seemed so excited that Nancy knew she had to say something. "I'm really happy your baking has been a hit," she said truthfully. "It does sound like a good opportunity. But are you sure you want to *move* here? I mean, maybe you could get a job baking back in River Heights."

"Ted wants me to stay on and work for him at the restaurant. Just think—me, Bess Marvin, pastry chef at Café de Carmel."

Nancy frowned as a thought occurred to her. Was it the job Bess found so exciting or the guy? Nancy didn't like the idea of her friend giving up everything she had in River Heights to spend time with a guy she had only known for a few weeks.

George had been listening to Bess's explanation, picking at imaginary pieces of lint on the blanket. Finally she said quietly, "I just can't imagine your living so far away, Bess."

"You can come visit. It's a perfect vacation spot. Don't you love it here?" Bess asked enthusiastically. "Walks on the beach, golf, shopping . . ."

Ted was watching them carefully, Nancy noticed. No wonder he was so possessive of Bess— he didn't want Nancy or George to talk Bess out of staying in Carmel.

"You don't seem very happy for me," Bess said.

"It's not that," Nancy said quickly. "It's just that you really surprised us with this news."

"You'll get used to it," Ted said. After picking up one of the plastic containers of food, he began to spoon potato salad onto the six plastic plates. "Why don't we eat?"

Obviously Ted considered the matter settled. Nancy decided to let the subject drop—but only for now. She didn't want to ruin the picnic for everyone.

George leaned close to Nancy. "We need to talk to Bess about this move," she whispered.

"Definitely," Nancy agreed. "Later, when we can discuss it privately."

Nancy's thoughts were still on Bess's proposed move an hour later as she made her way up Ocean Avenue to Marcia Cheung's jewelry store.

The picnic dinner had been delicious, but the mood was forced. Everyone had pretended to be happy, skirting the issue of Bess's move with smiles and small talk.

Nancy had been relieved when it was almost eight o'clock so she could excuse herself for her meeting with Marcia Cheung.

The sun had set during their beach picnic. As Nancy hurried up the hill, she saw that most of the stores were closed. There were a lot fewer tourists milling about than there had been during the day. The lights were still on in Cheung Original Designs, but a Closed sign hung in the window.

Nancy knocked softly, and a moment later Marcia appeared in the doorway between the showroom and the back room. Seeing Nancy, Marcia hurried to the door.

"Nancy?" she mouthed through the glass door.

Nancy nodded, then moved to the side so Marcia could open the door. "Thanks for waiting around."

"I had work to do, anyway," Marcia said softly. "Come on back into my workroom. Can I get you some coffee or a soda?"

"No, thanks. I just ate way too much dinner," Nancy said with a smile.

Marcia's room was dominated by a long, well-lit workbench with tools scattered on it. A desk covered with papers was pushed against the wall opposite the workbench, and a small safe sat in the far corner. There was a solid wood back door and no windows in the room.

"It's so nice of you to agree to help me," Marcia said, smiling shyly.

"You may not think so after I ask you a million questions," Nancy responded.

"Ask away," Marcia said with a nervous chuckle. She gestured for Nancy to sit on one of the two swivel chairs in front of the desk. She took the other one.

Nancy was surprised by Marcia's quiet manner. It was in such marked contrast to Len's explosiveness. The couple certainly seemed like a case of opposites attracting.

Nancy decided to start with small talk, hoping to put Marcia at ease. "How long have you had your own studio?" she asked.

"About six months," Marcia answered, "but I've been designing jewelry ever since I was a teenager. I majored in art at college, then went to work for Cy Baxter."

Nancy nodded. "I visited Mr. Baxter this afternoon. He didn't seem very happy about your opening up your own shop," she commented.

"He was furious!" Marcia exclaimed, rolling her eyes. "Then, when Joanna Burton asked me to design a necklace for her, Cy called and accused me of stealing his client," she added.

"Baxter told me that Miss Burton asked him to design the necklace first, but he wouldn't because she owed him money," Nancy said. Now she wondered if he'd been lying. He could have said that just to save face.

"I wish he'd said something to me about the money," Marcia said, sighing deeply. "Miss Burton still owes me a final payment, and I don't see how I can ask her for it now."

Giving Marcia an apologetic smile, Nancy said, "I'm afraid I don't know anything about how jewelry design works. You'll have to explain everything you did with the necklace before I can figure out who might have taken the diamonds."

"Okay," Marcia agreed. "First Miss Burton showed me the old necklace and said she wanted a new setting for the diamonds—there were a dozen stones," she began.

"Did she leave the old necklace with you then?" Nancy asked.

Marcia shook her head. "No, she took it back while I worked on the design for the new setting. That took about a week. After she approved the design, she brought the old necklace back and left it—that was on a Monday, I remember."

Nodding toward the safe, Marcia added, "The settings and diamonds were safely locked away every second I wasn't working on the necklace. I was finished with the new necklace by Friday, and Miss Burton picked it up the same day."

So Marcia had had the necklace for four days, Nancy thought, doing the arithmetic in her head. Marcia—or someone else—would definitely have had the time to switch the diamonds for fakes. Glancing at the desk, Nancy noticed a pile of bills. She glimpsed a red "past due" sticker on one of them.

If Marcia or Len needed money, that would give them an even bigger motive, Nancy reasoned. She couldn't rule out the possibility that someone else was involved—someone like Cy Baxter.

"You're positive the stones in the old necklace were real diamonds?" Nancy asked.

Marcia nodded emphatically. "They were real, all right. The only difference in the necklace Miss Burton brought in and the necklace she picked up was the setting. The old necklace was heavy with gold. My design emphasized the diamonds."

Marcia opened a drawer in the work desk and sifted through some files. Pulling a photograph from one of the files, she held it out to Nancy.

"This is beautiful," Nancy said. The necklace in the photo featured diamonds of different sizes set in a fanciful and elegant design. "Joanna Burton must have been very pleased with it."

"Len said she absolutely raved about it," Marcia said proudly.

"Len?" Nancy was surprised.

Marcia nodded. "I wasn't here when Joanna came to pick it up." Marcia's hands were moving constantly as she spoke, and Nancy glanced down to see what she was doing. Marcia had on a gold charm bracelet, which she turned around and around on her wrist.

"We saw charms just like those on your bracelet when we were at Cy Baxter's shop this afternoon," Nancy commented.

"They're all Cy Baxter charms," Marcia said, smiling. "Charms are his trademark. That's why I don't make them here. I didn't think it would be fair to him."

Nancy was impressed with Marcia's loyalty to the man. He obviously considered Marcia a traitor, though. The real question was, did Cy resent Marcia enough to set her up for diamond theft?

"Cy said he noticed scratches on the necklace when Joanna Burton brought it to him to be appraised," Nancy said, watching Marcia carefully for her reaction.

"Scratches?" Marcia was genuinely horrified. "I'm sure there weren't any when I left the necklace for Miss Burton."

"Could Len have made some adjustments before Joanna picked it up?" Nancy asked, glancing at all the tools lying around.

Marcia laughed. "Len would never touch a piece of jewelry. He's much more comfortable with a sledgehammer. It may not look hard, but setting jewels is delicate work requiring certain skills." With another laugh she added, "I assure you, Len definitely does *not* have those skills."

Len did seem to be the only one besides Marcia who'd had access to the necklace before it was returned to Joanna Burton, Nancy thought. Since Marcia hadn't been in the shop when the actress picked up the necklace, she couldn't know for sure that the necklace still had the real diamonds in it.

Nancy walked over to the back door and examined the lock. "Does anyone besides you have a key to the shop?" she asked.

"Len does, of course. Other than that, the rental company may have one. We added a security system monitored by a local company after we rented the shop. Jewelry stores are always a potential target for theft." Marcia showed Nancy the electronic panel beside the back door. A light on it was blinking red.

"What does the red light mean?" Nancy asked.

"That the alarm is off," Marcia explained. "When it's on, the light is green. This door leads into an alley, but we rarely use it. There's a second panel beside the front door. Every morning we enter a code to deactivate the system, and we activate it when we leave at night."

Nancy's gaze skimmed over the work area again. "Who has access to the safe?" she asked Marcia.

"Len and I are the only ones who know the combination."

Nancy had no more questions for the moment. She wanted to talk to Joanna Burton, though. The actress might be able to tell her if anyone else had access to the necklace.

When Nancy asked Marcia for Joanna Burton's telephone number, Marcia handed her a business card. "Len mentioned that you might need the number, so I wrote it down for you. The card has the number here at the store. And my home number is noted beneath it, in case you have any more questions."

Nancy glanced at her watch. It was past eight-thirty. "Can I use your phone to call Miss Burton? I'd like to try to set up an appointment with her before it gets too late."

"No problem," Marcia said. She gestured toward the phone on the desk. "We have two lines. One is for the jewelry shop, and one is for Len's landscaping business," she explained as she walked into the front room. Nancy punched in the numbers Marcia had written on the back of the card. The line was busy. Nancy leaned against the desk to wait.

Just then the doorknob on the back door rattled, startling Nancy. She froze, all her attention focused on the door. If it was Len, she'd expect to hear a key in the lock. Instead she heard a scraping against the wood.

Moving quickly to the door, Nancy pressed her ear against it and heard someone moving outside. She took a deep breath and unlocked the deadbolt. Then she slowly eased the door open and slipped outside.

Nancy gasped as a tall shape lunged out of the shadows at her. Before she could react, the figure had reached out and grabbed her!

Chapter

Five

Nancy screamed as her arms were pulled behind her and held in a grip of iron. She struggled to free herself, but her attacker was too strong.

"Marcia! Call for help!" Nancy shouted back into the building.

Footsteps raced into the workroom. "Morgan! It's okay," Nancy heard Marcia shout.

When Nancy was free to turn around and confront her attacker she found herself face-to-face with one of the handsomest men she'd ever seen. His eyes were a bright aqua blue, and his skin was perfectly tanned. His thick, wavy brown hair was streaked with sun-bleached highlights as if he spent a lot of time at the beach.

"Marcia, sorry," the man said in a deep,

resonant voice. "I was making my rounds, checking to make sure your door was locked, and then it was slowly pushed open. I thought whoever was coming out was sneaking out. Very sorry, miss," he said to Nancy.

"Nancy, this is Morgan Fowler. He works for Seaside Security, the company that monitors our alarm system," Marcia explained.

Morgan's eyes widened as he took in Nancy. "I don't think I've had the pleasure," he said, holding out his hand. When Nancy shook it, Morgan held on a little longer than he needed. "A friend of yours, Marcia?" he asked, never taking his eyes off Nancy.

"Nancy's staying at the Provence Inn. She's helping Len and me find out what happened to Joanna Burton's necklace. She's a detective," Marcia explained. Turning to Nancy, she added, "We've already talked to the security company about the necklace. They've assured us that there was no lapse in security. Neither the guards nor Len nor I noticed any sign of a break-in."

Morgan seemed to have heard only Marcia's first words. "So you're a detective?" he asked. "Perhaps you could use some help."

"Thanks for the offer, but I'm doing fine on my own," Nancy said pleasantly. She wasn't sure if he was being condescending, or if he was just flirting.

"Anyway, Morgan may not be working for Seaside much longer," Marcia put in. "He's an actor up for a movie role that it looks like he'll get."

So he was an actor, Nancy mused. She wasn't surprised. It seemed to her that Morgan had been performing since they'd met.

"As soon as the part comes through, I'm out of here," Morgan said smugly. "Still, I'll keep my eyes open." He gave Nancy and Marcia a two-finger salute, then walked back through the alley, whistling.

Nancy and Marcia went back inside the shop, and Marcia bolted the door behind them. Gathering up her purse and a large canvas tote bag, she asked Nancy, "Ready to go?"

"Sure. Joanna's line was busy, so I'll try when I get back to my room. I hope I can talk to her tomorrow," said Nancy.

She glanced around the workroom one more time, then followed Marcia to the front door. Marcia punched a code into the pad, activating the security system, then quickly locked the door. A green light indicated the system was on.

"Thanks again, Nancy. I'll be glad when this whole thing is cleared up. It makes me nervous when Len gets all worked up and goes around threatening people—even though I know he'd never carry out his threats. It's just his way."

Nancy's brow furrowed. "Threats? What is Len threatening to do?" she asked.

Marcia seemed embarrassed that she had brought up the subject. "Um, he said something about setting Joanna Burton straight, telling her that I had nothing to do with stealing her diamonds. But I talked him out of it and told him you'd take care of it," Marcia assured Nancy.

"Hmm," was all Nancy said, but inside she was worried. She couldn't really rule out Len or Marcia as suspects. After witnessing Len's temper, Nancy wasn't convinced that he would keep his anger under control. She only hoped he could.

"You're just in time for spiced cider," George said when Nancy walked into their room at the Provence Inn ten minutes later.

George was carrying a tray with three steaming mugs from the kitchenette to the small sitting area next to the beds. She set the tray down on the coffee table, then joined Bess on the couch.

"It's Ted's special recipe," Bess added.

Taking one of the mugs, Nancy sipped the steaming cider. "Mmm. That's really good," she said, taking it over to the phone.

"I need to call Joanna Burton to set up an appointment to see her," she told Bess and George.

Nancy took the card Marcia had given her from her purse and dialed the actress's number.

"Hello?"

Nancy felt a thrill as she recognized Joanna Burton's rich, sultry voice. "Miss Burton?" she asked to make sure.

"Yes, who's this?" Miss Burton said curtly.

"My name is Nancy Drew. I'm looking into the claim you've made that the diamonds in a piece of your jewelry were removed and replaced with fake stones."

"It's about time someone returned my call," Miss Burton snapped. "When will I get my check?"

It dawned on Nancy that Miss Burton must believe Nancy worked for the insurance company.

"Miss Burton, I, um, need to ask you a few questions about your claim," Nancy said, without actually telling the actress she *wasn't* with the insurance company. "Perhaps I could stop by your house tomorrow morning, about ten?"

Nancy heard Miss Burton let out a long sigh. "This won't take long?"

"I'll make it as quick as possible," Nancy promised.

"Tomorrow, then, ten A.M." Then the line went dead.

Nancy raised her eyes to see her friends staring at her in amazement. "You're going to Joanna Burton's house!" Bess exclaimed as Nancy hung up.

"It *is* pretty exciting," Nancy admitted. "Do you want to come along?"

"Not at ten in the morning," Bess said, disappointed. "I do my baking then."

Bess's comment suddenly reminded Nancy of Bess's proposed move to Carmel. For the past hour or so Nancy had been so caught up in the case that she'd forgotten about it. Now, Nancy decided, it was time to talk to Bess.

"Bess, about this job and staying here in Carmel," George began before Nancy could say anything.

"Isn't it great?" Bess asked, a dreamy expression in her eyes.

"We think it's great that things are going so well, but isn't this kind of sudden?" Nancy asked her. "Have you really been here long enough to know if you want to stay?" She hesitated before adding, "It's hard to tell if you're staying because of the job or because of Ted."

Bess bit her lower lip. "I guess it's a little of both," she admitted.

"Did you tell your mom and dad?" George wanted to know. "What did they say?"

"They were the ones who suggested I invite you two out here to talk about it. They're willing to go along with whatever I decide."

"We're not trying to talk you out of staying here, but whenever I think about you here and us in River Heights . . ." George didn't finish the sentence, but her sad expression said a lot.

"That would be the hardest part," Bess said softly, "being separated from you two and my family."

She opened her mouth to say something else

but was cut off as the phone rang. Nancy reached over and picked it up.

"Hello?"

"Nancy, it's Mrs. Menendez. Someone left a package for you at the desk. Do you want to come get it, or shall I send it along?"

"A package?" Nancy couldn't imagine who would be sending her something there. "I'll come get it," she told Mrs. Menendez.

"I need to pick up a package someone left for me at the desk," she told Bess and George.

"A secret admirer?" George teased. "Is there something you aren't telling us, Nan?"

Nancy giggled. "So far he's been so secret that even *I* don't know about him. I'll be right back, guys."

She went down the hall and staircase to the inn's reception area.

"I came out to the desk a few minutes ago, and this package was sitting here," Mrs. Menendez said, pointing to a cardboard box on the counter. "I guess whoever sent it wants to remain anonymous."

The box had Nancy's name printed on the outside, but there was nothing to indicate from where or from whom it had come. "Thanks," Nancy told Mrs. Menendez.

As soon as Nancy stepped back inside her room Bess said, "Open it!"

"Who even knows you're staying here?" George wondered aloud.

Nancy asked herself the same question. She quickly ripped off the tape holding the cardboard lid down and pulled the flaps open.

"Oh, no!" Bess exclaimed, staring into the box.

Nancy's stomach churned as she gazed down at the smashed cuckoo clock that lay in the box. The cuckoo lay crushed outside the clock's little door. A sheet of paper was affixed to its pointy beak. Written on the paper in block letters were the words "Time to mind your own business."

Chapter

Six

FOR A LONG MOMENT Nancy, Bess, and George stared at the smashed cuckoo clock in shocked silence.

"I can't believe someone is threatening you," George finally said, her brown eyes worried.

"I don't like this, Nancy," Bess added. She stepped away from the box and flopped down on George's bed. "What if whoever sent this tries to hurt you? Maybe you should drop the case. I'm sure Marcia would understand."

"There's no way I'm going to back off now," Nancy said firmly.

Reaching into the box, George removed the clock and tried to stick the bird back inside the door. "You guys, this looks like the clock we saw at Cy Baxter's store!" she said excitedly. "Who-

ever it was must have found out who you really
are and sent it to scare you off."

"Maybe," Nancy said, frowning. "But why
would he send me one of his own clocks? I mean,
he would have to know that I would make the
connection between the cuckoo clock and
him—"

Nancy broke off as someone pounded on the
door. She tensed automatically. Bess and George
also froze, their eyes turned to Nancy.

"It's probably nothing, you guys," Nancy said
as she peered through the peephole. "It's Ted,"
she announced, smiling.

The first thing Nancy noticed when she opened
the door was the scowl on Ted's face.

"Is Bess still here?" he asked, pushing a hand
back through his straight dark hair.

"I'm here," Bess called, getting up from
George's bed.

"I went to your room to talk about the desserts
for the weekend," Ted said. "When you weren't
there, I thought I'd try here. Are you going to be a
lot longer?"

His gaze fell on the broken cuckoo clock.
"What happened to that?"

Ted listened while Bess, George, and Nancy
showed him the threatening note. He seemed so
concerned that Nancy almost forgave him his
attitude toward Bess.

"Wow. This is turning into a pretty hairy

50

situation," Ted said. "I hope you can find out who's responsible, Nancy."

Before Nancy could respond, Ted turned to Bess. "So, about those desserts—" he began.

"Well, we were just talking, but if it's really important . . ." Bess glanced at Nancy and George.

"Go ahead, Bess," Nancy said, trying to sound as if she didn't mind. "We can finish talking tomorrow."

"Thanks, guys. What can I say? He just can't be without me for a minute," Bess said, giggling.

Nancy and George said good night.

"I'm not sure what it is about that guy I don't like," George said after the door had closed on Bess and Ted.

"He sure doesn't want Bess to spend time with us. Then again, maybe we're just jealous because he might take Bess away from us."

"Can you believe that Bess got up and left for the restaurant before seven in the morning?" George asked the following morning as she and Nancy jogged along the beach. "I'm in shock!"

"I know what you mean. Bess isn't exactly the early-bird type," Nancy agreed with a laugh. "If she's willing to get up at this hour, she must really love her job!"

Nancy and George had gotten up early to go running. When they passed by Mrs. Menendez in the lobby, Ted's mother had told them that Bess had already gone to the café.

"Well, at least Bess promised to finish early so we can get in some sightseeing this afternoon," Nancy said, lengthening her stride to keep up with George. She tucked a flyaway strand of reddish blond hair beneath her headband and breathed in the moist, salty ocean air.

The day was bright and clear. A brisk breeze blew in from the ocean, sending waves beating against the dark rocks that rose along the shoreline.

"Anyway, you and I will be busy meeting Joanna Burton this morning," George said. "I'm totally psyched!"

Nancy grinned at her friend. "Me, too. Who wouldn't be excited to meet a movie star?"

The girls finished their run, then showered and dressed. Nancy wanted to look official for her meeting with the actress, so she put on a lavender suit with a wrap skirt and a top in a complementary shade.

After breakfast Nancy and George headed out and got in their rental car. Following the directions Mrs. Menendez had given them, they headed for Seventeen-Mile Drive.

"There's the entrance," George said a few minutes later.

Up ahead Nancy saw a wooden gate house. As she pulled to a halt in front of it, a security guard stepped out and smiled.

"Good morning, ladies," he greeted them. "There's a fee to enter the drive."

After Nancy had paid him, the guard handed Nancy a receipt and a brochure with a map showing all the sights of interest. Nancy handed the brochure to George.

"Hmm. It says here that Joanna Burton's house is about a mile and a half down the drive," George said, consulting the pamphlet. "It has a black iron gate."

Nancy nodded. "I'm glad we got the map. Otherwise we might not have found the right house."

Nancy drove into a wooded area. The houses were large and built much farther apart than the ones in town. Nancy couldn't sightsee, though, because it took all her attention to negotiate the narrow, curved road.

"Whoa! Look at that!" George exclaimed as they emerged from the wooded area.

Nancy slowed the car and pulled into an overlook just ahead. When she finally checked out the view, she was stunned.

A panoramic ocean scene stretched before them. The rocky beach was far below, at the foot of a long, sandy hill. Beyond the sand the blue waters were dotted with sailboats and windsurfers.

"That's Monterey Bay," George informed Nancy, referring to the map in her lap.

"I feel as if we got our money's worth just

looking at the scenery," Nancy said. "But we'd better go. It's almost ten."

Putting the car in drive, Nancy pulled back on to the road. They continued to travel with the ocean to their right; sometimes they were at sea level, sometimes on a ridge high up.

"Joanna Burton's house can't be much farther," Nancy said, slowing as they approached a curve.

She was just easing into the turn when a white pickup truck came roaring around the curve from the opposite direction. It was halfway in Nancy's lane, heading straight at the girls' car!

"Nancy, look out!" George cried. Her face was white as she grabbed the dashboard.

Nancy instinctively jerked the car to the right to avoid a collision. In that instant she got a dizzying glimpse of the rocky beach and water far below. She heard George gasp as she slammed on the brakes and spun the wheel to the left and away from the cliff's edge.

The wheels screeched as the car skidded out of control. Nancy felt the bump as the car jumped onto the narrow shoulder.

They were headed toward the edge of the drop-off!

Chapter

Seven

Nᴀɴᴄʏ's ʜᴇᴀʀᴛ ʟᴇᴀᴘᴛ into her throat as she pulled the wheel left with all her strength and continued to pump the brakes. Please, *please* don't go over the edge! she begged silently.

For one awful moment the car continued to skid toward the cliff's edge. Then the brakes finally held, and the car shuddered to a stop.

Nancy's legs felt like jelly as she backed onto the road and drove to the next overlook. She pulled in and parked beside an empty car. Falling forward, she rested her head against the steering wheel and took in deep breaths of air to still her pounding heart.

"That was a close one," George said, slowly relaxing her grip on the dashboard. After opening her purse George fumbled around in it.

"That truck had a logo painted on the side—a

pine tree, very stylized," she said, pulling out an envelope and a pen. With a shaky hand she began to sketch a pine tree, its branches curved and capped with white, like ocean waves.

"I couldn't read the name, but I figure someone will know who the truck belongs to if we show them this picture," George continued, holding the drawing out to Nancy. "It makes me really mad when people drive so recklessly. I'm turning this guy in."

"It was a guy?" Nancy asked. "I didn't have time to glance at the driver. It took everything I had just to keep the car on the road."

"To tell you the truth, I'm really not sure," George said. She smiled weakly. "That was pretty fancy driving, Drew."

Nancy shuddered at the thought of what might have happened if the car had continued its slide off the road. She took another deep breath, then checked her watch. "We'd better get going. It's ten o'clock now."

Checking for traffic, Nancy pulled back onto the road. A few moments later George pointed and said, "That must be Joanna Burton's. See those black wrought-iron gates?"

Just up ahead Nancy saw the iron gates. She pulled up in front of them to lean out the window and press the intercom button. When there was no answer, she pressed again.

"Maybe this thing doesn't work," she said.

Getting out of the car, Nancy tested the gate. It

was locked. Once more she tried the intercom. "Miss Burton? It's Nancy Drew," she said into the speaker, although there was no indication that she'd made a connection. After waiting a few more minutes, she tried again. No answer once more.

Just then a small, fluffy white dog raced up to the fence, poked its nose through the iron bars, and started yapping loudly.

"What a darling dog!" George exclaimed, getting out of the car and squatting down in front of it. The dog ceased its racket, sniffed George's hand, and began to whine.

"Something's not right," Nancy said, looking through the gate at the house. "We had an appointment with Miss Burton. And this dog almost seems scared—"

The piercing sound of an approaching siren interrupted Nancy's thoughts, and in the next minute a small white car with flashing lights pulled up behind their car.

Nancy was surprised to see Morgan Fowler get out of the car. "Could I see some identification, please?" he asked.

"Morgan, it's Nancy Drew. We met last night, remember?" Nancy said. "Marcia Cheung introduced us. This is my friend George Fayne."

Recognition shone in Morgan's aqua eyes. "Nancy. The detective?" Morgan let go with one of his smiles. Holding out his hand to George, he said, "Nice to meet you."

Then his expression grew serious. "One of the neighbors called in to report two loiterers at Miss Burton's gate. Part of our service is to make sure no one bothers our clients," Morgan said.

"Nancy had an appointment to meet with Miss Burton, but the intercom isn't working, and the gate's locked," George explained.

"You must be pulling a double shift," Nancy said as Morgan tried the intercom button, too. "Last night and again this morning?"

Morgan nodded. "We rotate days, evenings, nights. I got stuck with a shift change without any time off in between," he said.

A third car, a sleek silver sports car, pulled up, then stopped. A tall woman with red hair done up in a smart French twist stepped out of the car. She was dressed in a navy suit and a red silk blouse. "What's going on here?" she asked, her hazel eyes flitting from Morgan to the two girls.

"Stephanie! What a nice surprise." Morgan quickly held out his hand to the attractive woman.

Stephanie ignored the outstretched hand. "Who are these people?"

Nancy wondered the same thing about Stephanie. Who was she to be asking so many questions? And how did Morgan know her? Judging from her expensive clothes, Stephanie wasn't household help. Perhaps she was Miss Burton's lawyer.

Morgan quickly introduced Nancy and

George. "They had an appointment this morning with Joanna. But the intercom isn't working, and the gate's locked," he explained.

"Open it," Stephanie told him.

"I'm not supposed to do that," Morgan said, hesitating.

"Something could have happened to Joanna. Open the gate," Stephanie insisted.

Morgan leaned in and removed a clipboard from his car. He flipped through the papers, then went back to the gate and punched some numbers into the keypad set into it. The iron doors opened.

Without so much as a glance at anyone else, Stephanie got into her sports car and drove through. Nancy quickly jumped into her car and followed before anyone could tell her not to. George stopped and picked up the dog, carrying it with her up to the house.

The house was Spanish style with a red-tile roof and dark red trim, Nancy saw when she joined George at the front door. She was surprised to note that the paint on the trim was peeling.

"What do you need to see my client about?" Stephanie asked, appearing next to Nancy and George.

"I'm investigating a claim Miss Burton made regarding a diamond necklace," Nancy said.

"Are you with the insurance company?" Stephanie asked.

Nancy didn't want to lie, but she had no reason to tell this woman anything, either. "I'm sorry, but I don't believe I caught your name," Nancy said, dodging the question.

"This is Stephanie Cooke, Nancy," Morgan supplied. He had driven his car inside the gates, too. "You've probably heard of her. She's Joanna's agent—one of the best in Hollywood."

Stephanie gave the girls a stiff smile before ringing the front bell. When no one answered, she tried the door, but it was locked. "I drove all the way here from L.A. this morning. Joanna didn't say a word about going out, and she usually tells me everything," Stephanie said, obviously concerned.

"I don't have a key to the door," Morgan said.

Stephanie poked in her purse. "I don't have mine with me, either." Stephanie pressed her lips together, then turned and headed for the garage. "I think I know where she keeps an extra key hidden. Let me go in and see what's going on."

"Maybe I'd better call this in to Seaside Security," Morgan said, shifting nervously from one foot to the other.

Stephanie waved away the idea. "Let's check it out ourselves first in case she's just sleeping in."

The agent disappeared around the corner of the house, and a few minutes later the front door opened and Stephanie appeared. "There was a key in the garage," she announced.

"Doesn't Miss Burton have a housekeeper or

something?" Nancy asked as they stepped into the foyer. "This is an awfully large house for her to take care of by herself."

"A woman comes in a couple of times a week to clean," Stephanie said. "Joanna doesn't need full-time help."

The agent pointed to a set of French Doors at the opposite end of a huge sunken living room. "Why don't you three go out on the terrace and wait?" she said in a tone that left no room for argument. "There's a wonderful view. I'll find Joanna and tell her you're here." With that, Stephanie disappeared up a set of stairs.

As Nancy stepped down into the living room she saw that it was much less lavish than she had expected. The main feature was a stone fireplace that dominated one wall. The rest of the room was sparsely furnished in a style that Nancy remembered had been popular a number of years earlier. The furniture was in good shape but a little dated.

Morgan remained inside while Nancy opened the French doors and stepped out onto the terrace. George followed, still holding the fluffy white dog that had run up to them at the gate. The dog jumped out of George's arms as soon as she walked outside.

"Check out this view!" George exclaimed softly.

Nancy had to agree that it was spectacular. A set of steps was cut into the hillside leading down to a small crescent of beach. Beyond, the ocean stretched as far as the eye could see, sparkling in the bright sunlight.

Glancing back into the house, Nancy saw that Stephanie had returned to the living room and was now deep in conversation with Morgan.

"It looks as if Joanna's been here this morning," George said. She had stepped up to a glass-topped table shaded by a red umbrella. "Here's a carafe of coffee and two cups with coffee in them."

Nancy touched one of the cups. "It's still warm," she said. "So where's Miss Burton? And who was drinking coffee with her?"

Something about the scene made Nancy very uneasy. The dog was still edgy and whined as it sniffed around the terrace.

"Nancy, look down there, over by those rocks. Are those sea otters?" George asked.

Following George's gaze, Nancy spotted the brown animals swimming among the rocks. "They're adorable," Nancy said, her mind still on Joanna Burton.

"Let's go take a closer look at the otters," George said, starting down the steep steps. "Maybe Joanna Burton went for a walk on the beach, and we'll run into her."

Nancy hesitated. "Okay." She finally gave in. "But let's go for just a minute, okay?"

George was halfway down the steps when she

stopped suddenly, causing Nancy to bump into her.

"Uh, no!" George exclaimed. There was no mistaking the note of alarm in her voice. "Nancy, look down there." She pointed down to the beach at the foot of the wooden staircase.

The first thing Nancy saw was a swirl of hot pink fabric. Then she caught sight of the dark hair and the outstretched, immobile hand.

The realization hit her in a sickening flash. A woman's body lay crumpled at the bottom of the steps!

Chapter
Eight

Nancy's stomach twisted into a tight knot as she stared down at the inert form. All at once she leapt into action.

"Quick. Go get Stephanie and Morgan, and then phone for help," she said to George.

As George eased past Nancy back up the stairs Nancy hurried down to the beach. When she reached the sand she definitely recognized Joanna Burton's lovely features, with her high, delicate brows. There was no blood on her, but the woman's neck was bent at an odd angle. Just looking at it made Nancy's stomach flip.

Kneeling beside the actress, Nancy felt for a pulse. There was none.

She sat back on her heels and took a deep breath. "Stay calm, Drew," she told herself. It wasn't easy. The actress's dog had followed Nancy down the stairs and was now whining pitifully.

Trying not to look at Joanna Burton's neck, Nancy quickly looked for some clue to what had happened. The side seam of the actress's beach wrap was ripped and hanging loose at one side. Her right hand was tightly clenched, but Nancy couldn't tell if she was holding anything in it.

Nancy jumped as a scream rang out from above her, quickly followed by muffled sobs. Looking up, she saw Morgan, his arm around Stephanie, standing at the top of the steps. George was halfway down the stairs.

"Is she–" George called down, somehow knowing the answer.

Nancy nodded grimly. Brushing the sand off her knees, she slowly stood up.

"Morgan called the police and an ambulance," George said. "What do you think happened?"

"I'm not sure. It looks as if she fell down the stairs. Her beach wrap is torn, though, which makes me think there might have been a struggle," Nancy said. "I think she's holding something, but we have to wait for the police to check it out."

George picked up the dog again and cuddled it close to her body. She and Nancy were both somber as they climbed up the steps to the house. Morgan and Stephanie had moved into the living room.

"I should have gotten here earlier," Stephanie murmured, staring out through the French Doors at the ocean. "Joanna called me last night. She said that Marcia Cheung had phoned, wanting to talk to her about that necklace. I told her not to say one word to her, to let the police handle it."

"You think Marcia had something to do with this?" Nancy asked. She couldn't imagine Marcia killing anyone.

"I wouldn't jump to conclusions, Stephanie," Morgan said nervously. "Joanna could have tripped and fallen down the steps."

Nancy suddenly remembered the two cups on the terrace. "Do you know if anyone else was visiting Miss Burton this morning?" she asked Stephanie. "There are two cups on the patio table, and the coffee in them is still warm."

"All I know is that Marcia wanted to see her," Stephanie replied. "Joanna said she was frightened because Marcia seemed so angry."

Marcia, angry? That didn't sound like the same person Nancy had met the night before. Nancy would have to check into Stephanie's claim.

"Did Joanna mention that anyone else had talked to her?" Nancy asked.

Stephanie shook her head.

Before Nancy could ask her next question, sirens announced the arrival of the police and ambulance. Morgan hurried to answer the intercom.

Nancy recognized the first person who entered. It was the woman she and George had seen at Marcia's store the day before. The woman walked into the living room followed by two uniformed officers and two paramedics carrying a stretcher. Morgan followed them in, then stationed himself beside the French doors.

The woman introduced herself as Detective Bommarito, then asked everyone else to stay put while she and her crew went down to Miss Burton's body. When the detective returned she spoke briefly to Morgan Fowler in hushed tones. Nancy heard the words "broken neck."

After a moment the detective came over to where Nancy, George, and Stephanie were waiting in the living room. "Were any of you present when Miss Burton fell?" Detective Bommarito asked them.

They all shook their heads.

"This is Nancy Drew and her friend George Fayne," Morgan said to the detective. "They came here to talk to Joanna about her necklace. Nancy's a detective. She's working for Marcia Cheung."

"A detective?" Detective Bommarito's eyes narrowed. She was anything but impressed.

"And this is Stephanie Cooke, Joanna's agent," Morgan went on, moving over to Stephanie. The agent's face was tear-streaked. A few tendrils of red hair had come loose from her

French twist and were hanging in frizzy strands around her face.

Stephanie took a deep breath, then spoke in a numb voice. "Joanna called me last night. She was worried because Marcia kept calling to talk to her about the necklace. I told her not to talk to Marcia until I got here."

"What time did Miss Burton call you, Stephanie?" Nancy asked.

"What time?" Stephanie repeated. "It was late. I'm not really sure."

Something about what Stephanie had said didn't make sense to Nancy. Marcia knew Nancy intended to see Joanna Burton. Why would she call herself?

"Do you know if Miss Burton's beach wrap was torn before today?" Detective Bommarito asked.

Stephanie shook her head adamantly. "Joanna would never have worn anything that wasn't in perfect condition. She just wouldn't."

"What about this?" Detective Bommarito asked, holding up a plastic bag. "Miss Burton was clutching it in her hand. Do you recognize it?"

The bag contained a gold sea otter charm, Nancy saw. Connected to the charm was a twisted, broken loop that had probably attached the charm to a bracelet.

Again Stephanie shook her head. "It doesn't belong to Joanna."

With a start, Nancy remembered that Marcia had a bracelet full of gold charms. Nancy couldn't remember if Marcia had a sea otter or not, but she knew she had to tell the police.

"Marcia Cheung has a charm bracelet," Nancy told the detective. "I saw it last night."

"And Cy Baxter makes charms just like that in his jewelry store," George added.

Detective Bommarito made some notations in the notebook she carried. "Obviously, I'm going to have to ask them both some questions. It looks like someone is missing a charm from a bracelet. And there's a good chance that that person is responsible for Joanna Burton's death."

The detective had just confirmed Nancy's worst suspicion. Joanna Burton hadn't fallen down the stairs. She had been pushed.

"I can't believe Joanna Burton has been murdered," George said solemnly as she and Nancy drove back toward downtown Carmel.

"Not only that, but it looks as if both Marcia and Cy Baxter are suspects," Nancy said, frowning. "I'm not sure why either of them would kill her, unless she found out that one of them had stolen her diamonds. I definitely want to talk to Marcia about this right away."

"From what you said, Marcia doesn't seem like the violent type at all," George said. "Len is the one with the bad temper."

Nancy blinked and suddenly recalled a remark

Marcia had made the night before. "Marcia said something about that last night. Apparently Len threatened to confront Joanna Burton and 'set her straight.'"

George shot Nancy a worried glance. "What if *he's* the one who pushed her down the steps?" Then she shook herself. "Oh—but that doesn't make sense. Len wouldn't have had on a charm bracelet."

Nancy barely noticed the scenery on the drive back into town. Her mind was swirling with questions. Who had been drinking coffee with Joanna Burton? Who else besides Cy Baxter and Marcia Cheung had Baxter's charms? Did Joanna's death have anything to do with the stolen diamonds? And how did the smashed cuckoo clock fit in with all of this? Nancy hoped she could find some answers soon.

As soon as Nancy parked the car she and George headed straight for Marcia's shop. When they walked in the door, Marcia came hurrying in from the back room. She smiled when she saw Nancy and George.

"Did you talk to Miss Burton?" Marcia asked hopefully. Pale and tired-looking, she had dark circles under her eyes.

Nancy watched Marcia carefully as she told her the news of the actress's death.

"Dead?" Marcia whispered, her dark eyes widening. "How?" Her right hand grasped her left wrist. Then she glanced down, frowning.

Nancy followed Marcia's gaze. "Where's your bracelet?" she asked.

"I don't know." Marcia continued to stare at her bare wrist. "I guess I didn't put it on this morning. I left home so early." She opened a drawer under the counter, then pushed it shut. "No, I remember putting it on, because I took it off when I got here. I was doing some sketches, and it was getting in the way. Maybe it's in the workroom—"

Marcia turned to check back in the workroom. Nancy and George followed. "Maybe I didn't put it on this morning after all," she decided after a thorough search.

"The police think that Joanna was pushed down the stairs," Nancy said, fixing Marcia with a sober gaze. "She was holding a charm in her hand when we found her."

Marcia stared blankly at Nancy, then sat down in a chair. "You don't think—I wouldn't—I couldn't—"

"Joanna Burton's agent, Stephanie Cooke, claims that Miss Burton said you were calling and annoying her, asking to come see her about the necklace," George added.

"Why would I do that?" Marcia asked, confused. "You were going to talk to her, so why would I?"

Nancy raised a question. "You didn't go out to Miss Burton's this morning?"

"I—I was with a client here at the store this

morning, working on a design," Marcia replied. Nancy noticed that her eyes shifted nervously and couldn't help wondering if the young woman was hiding something.

Before she could ask Marcia anything else, the front door to the shop opened. "Hello?" a woman's voice called out.

"I'll go see what it's about," George offered.

Through the open doorway Nancy heard the woman inquire about a bracelet she'd left to be repaired. "I came by at ten-fifteen to pick it up, but the shop wasn't open yet," the woman was saying.

Nancy glanced at Marcia with narrowed eyes. "I thought you said you were here this morning," Nancy said in a low voice.

"Well, I wasn't at Joanna's. That's all you need to know," Marcia said. Turning away from Nancy, she went into the shop.

Nancy watched as Marcia retrieved a package from under the counter and held it out to the woman. "Your bracelet is ready, Mrs. Ortiz."

This case is getting more complicated every second, Nancy thought. Marcia had seemed genuinely surprised by the news of Joanna's murder. Either she was a very good actress or she was telling the truth and hadn't been there. But if she hadn't been at the actress's home, why wouldn't she say where she had been?

After Mrs. Ortiz had left, Marcia came out from behind the counter. Instead of rejoining

Nancy in the workroom, Marcia went to the front door. "I don't feel like answering any more questions," she said, her lips trembling. "I think you two should go now."

Nancy was irritated now. "Marcia, you and Len asked for my help. But I can't work for you if you don't tell me everything," she said.

Marcia let out a long sigh before looking at Nancy. "Please, I need some time to think this through," she said wearily. "Could you come back later?" She must have seen the disapproval in Nancy's face, because she quickly added, "Look, I didn't kill Joanna, but I can't talk about it now."

Marcia opened the shop door and stood there. Nancy didn't have any choice but to leave.

"I'll be back later," Nancy said to Marcia, but the door had already been shut, cutting off her words.

George rolled her eyes. "Talk about weird!" she said. "Well, we might as well see if Bess is done working." George started across the street.

Nancy automatically checked for traffic on Ocean Avenue. She noticed Len about half a block down the hill at the corner, talking to a dark-haired woman who looked vaguely familiar. Nancy lingered on the sidewalk a moment, hoping the woman would turn so she could identify her.

Len was speaking intently to the woman. Finally he handed her what appeared to be a small envelope. The woman glanced around warily before she stuffed the envelope in her pocket.

Something about their furtive behavior aroused Nancy's suspicions. Suddenly Len glanced up the hill, and his eyes landed on Nancy. He quickly looked away and said something to his companion. A moment later he moved briskly away, turning down a side street.

What was going on? Nancy wondered. Why did Len become so nervous when he saw her?

Nancy started toward the corner, hoping to catch up with Len. She had taken only a few steps when the woman Len had been talking to turned in Nancy's direction. Nancy immediately recognized her.

It was Cy Baxter's assistant!

Chapter

Nine

NANCY'S MIND RACED. What secretive business could those two have together? Could it somehow be related to Joanna Burton's death?

Nancy recalled the smashed cuckoo clock. Maybe the assistant had sent it. Nancy took off down Ocean Avenue toward the woman.

"Nancy, where are you going?" George called from across the street.

Nancy motioned for George to come with her, then turned back to look at the dark-haired woman. She had disappeared!

Nancy ran to the corner. Shading her eyes with her hand, she glanced in both directions, then frowned. Neither Len nor Cy Baxter's assistant was in sight.

"What's going on?" George asked breathlessly, catching up with Nancy.

"When we came out of Marcia's shop, Len was standing down here, talking to the woman we saw in Cy Baxter's shop yesterday," Nancy explained. "Len handed her a package, but when they saw me, they both hurried off."

She crossed her arms over her chest, trying to fit the pieces of information she had together. "Do you think it's possible that she and Len worked together to steal the diamonds from Joanna Burton's necklace?" she wondered out loud. "Len could have taken the necklace from the safe without Marcia knowing about it. Then he could have given the necklace to the woman to make the switch. She has access to all the right tools at Cy Baxter's store. And she must know where to get cubic zirconia."

"It's possible," George agreed. "I mean, Len did say they've been working hard to get their businesses off the ground. Maybe he stole the diamonds because money is tight." Then she frowned, running a hand through her short, dark curls. "But the diamond switch happened days ago. I still don't get what Len could be handing over to that woman now."

Nancy had been wondering the same thing. "It's possible there was money in the envelope. Maybe Len gave her a cut after he sold the diamonds."

Nancy absently fingered the hem of her blazer. "Let's face it. Marcia, Len, Cy Baxter, and his assistant are all still suspects, and we're no closer to figuring out who's guilty than we were yesterday."

George flicked a thumb back in the direction of the Café de Carmel. "Well, let's give up for now and see if Bess is through working. Maybe we can get in some sightseeing," she suggested. "After a break, maybe all of this will seem a little clearer."

"Mmm," Nancy said noncommittally. "I want to go back to Baxter's jewelry store, though. I want to check out both Baxter and his assistant more."

"*After* lunch," George insisted, pulling Nancy toward Café de Carmel. "All we've been through this morning has made me hungry!"

When the two girls entered Ted's restaurant, there was already a sizable lunch crowd. Libby, the waitress Bess had spoken to the day before, was rushing around taking orders and delivering food.

"I guess Bess is in the kitchen," George commented.

Just then the door to the kitchen opened and Ted emerged, a welcoming smile on his face. As soon as he recognized Nancy and George his smile faded.

"Hi," Nancy said brightly, ignoring his unfriendly expression.

"Uh, hi. Did you find anything out at Joanna Burton's this morning?" he asked. His question was polite enough, but Nancy knew he wasn't happy to see her and George.

Nancy smiled at him and said, "I thought we could fill you and Bess in at the same time. Is she here?"

"Bess is busy," he said curtly.

"Come on, you're the boss. Tell her she can take a break," George teased.

Ted just glowered at George. "She's not here right now," he told her. "She went to get stuff for a new dessert she wants to try."

What was with this guy? Nancy wondered. He was acting as if it were a crime even to ask about Bess. "So I guess that means she's not going to be able to go sightseeing with us this afternoon?" Nancy asked.

"Bess and I have a business to run," Ted said. "She said to tell you that she'll catch up with you when she has time." With that he disappeared back into the kitchen.

George turned to Nancy, angry red spots coloring her cheeks. "She'll catch up with us when she has time?" George said, keeping her voice low. "Bess *asked* us to come here. She's hardly had time to say hi since we arrived."

"I doubt that's the exact message she left for us," Nancy said, frowning. "I have a feeling Ted interpreted it more harshly."

"He isn't exactly Mr. Charming, is he?" George muttered. "Suddenly I'm not hungry. Let's get out of here."

Nancy nodded. "We can grab a slice of pizza or

something. And then let's go over to Cy Baxter's."

Baxter's Fine Jewelry seemed to be deserted when Nancy and George entered the shop forty-five minutes later.

"Where is everyone?" George murmured, stepping up to the counter.

Nancy shrugged and started toward the doorway that led to the back. From the doorway she caught sight of the assistant, who was studying a piece of jewelry on the table in front of her. She was so intent on her work that she didn't appear to hear Nancy and George at all.

Nancy held a finger up to her lips for silence, then stepped a little closer. She was trying to get a better look at the piece of jewelry. Could it be Marcia Cheung's charm bracelet?

As Nancy shifted her weight a floorboard let out a loud creak. The woman's head jerked up, and she gasped when she saw Nancy in the doorway. A split-second later she swept the piece of jewelry into a drawer. The jingly sound Nancy heard immediately made her think it was a charm bracelet.

"Can I help you?" she asked nervously. She hurried over to the doorway.

Nancy turned as the front door opened again and Cy Baxter strode into the shop. His eyes landed on Nancy and George and flickered with recognition.

"Rachel, why is there a customer in the work-room?" Baxter asked. Nancy wasn't actually in the workroom, but he obviously wasn't pleased to see her in the doorway.

"I'm sorry, Mr. Baxter," Rachel said. "I didn't hear her come in until just now."

Smiling at Nancy and George, Cy said, "So, have you decided to have me design your brace-let?" he asked.

It took Nancy a moment to remember what he was talking about. She'd almost forgotten that she'd pretended to be a customer during her last visit. This time she decided not to play games.

"Mr. Baxter, I'm investigating your claims about Joanna Burton's diamond necklace for Marcia Cheung," Nancy told him.

Cy Baxter's smile faded. "I don't have to answer any of your questions," he said. "And I'm certainly going to speak to Joanna about you. I don't see any reason why she should cooperate with you, either."

Nancy was surprised to hear him mention Joanna's name. Apparently he hadn't heard what had happened to her yet. Then again, there hadn't been much time for the news to get around, "Mr. Baxter, Joanna Burton died this morning," she said softly.

The jeweler blinked, and his hand went to his chest. "Joanna—dead?" he echoed.

Rachel was just as surprised. Her face turned a pasty, unhealthy color. "But—how?"

Nancy took a deep breath before answering. "She fell down her terrace steps. The police suspect she may have been pushed. When they found her she was holding a charm—a sea otter charm, like the ones you make."

"One of my charms?" Baxter asked weakly.

Nancy nodded, then asked her next question. She had a feeling Baxter wasn't going to like it. "Where have you been all morning?" she inquired.

Baxter opened his mouth to speak, but all that came out were sputtering noises. "Why are you asking me?" he finally demanded.

"You sell charms like the one the police found in Miss Burton's hand," George answered.

"I sell charms, but I don't wear them. And I assure you I was nowhere near Joanna Burton's house this morning," Baxter said defensively. "My Jaguar stalled when I was driving to work this morning. I had to have it towed all the way to the dealership in Monterey. The mechanics there are the only ones I trust. Monterey Imports—you can call them if you don't believe me."

His alibi would be easy to check, Nancy thought. She doubted that he was lying. "Do you know who else might have visited her?" she asked. "Someone who wears one of your bracelets?"

"I really couldn't say," Baxter replied. "Joanna Burton loved my charms. She gave them as gifts all the time."

"What about the charm bracelet your assistant was working on when we came in?" Nancy knew it was a long shot but hoped it would work.

"Yes," George said, picking up on Nancy's reasoning. "If you don't mind, we'd like to see if there's a sea otter missing from it."

Baxter appeared completely baffled. "Charm bracelet?" He turned to Rachel and asked, "What's this all about?"

Rachel looked panicky, and all the fight seemed to go out of her. Stepping over to the workbench where she'd been sitting before, she sank onto the stool.

Cy Baxter stood next to her while she opened the drawer in the work desk.

"What's this?" he asked, picking up a photograph of a man from the desktop.

Nancy moved closer to see who it was and immediately recognized Michael Davis. He was an older actor who was enjoying a comeback following the release of his latest movie.

Something was written on the back of the photo, Nancy noticed. Apparently Baxter saw it, too. He flipped the picture over and read, "'Rachel—In every future there is a past.' And it's signed." He laid the photo down in front of Rachel, shaking his head. "Honestly, Rachel. This is a place of business. It's unprofessional to keep pictures of movie stars piled on your desk."

When Rachel saw the photograph, her face went completely white. "Oh, no!" she murmured. Then she added, "I-I'm sorry, Mr. Baxter. I promise I'll get rid of it."

"Good. Now, where's that bracelet?" Baxter asked, getting back to business.

Rachel opened her work desk drawer and slowly took out a charm bracelet. "Len wanted me to put on the charm that you made for him—the one that's the logo from his landscaping business."

George stepped forward to look at the bracelet. "So that's what Nancy saw Len give you a little while ago?"

Rachel nodded. "He wanted it to be a surprise. Please don't tell Marcia."

Taking the charm bracelet from his assistant, Cy Baxter carefully examined it. "Here's Marcia's sea otter," he said, holding out the charm for Nancy to see.

Nancy carefully inspected the small gold loop connecting the charm to the bracelet. It was slightly tarnished, not shiny the way it would be if it were new. "Are you sure the sea otter charm was on there when Len gave the bracelet to you?" Nancy asked. "You didn't put that one on today?"

"Oh, no," Rachel answered with a firm shake of her head. "The only new charm is the logo of Len's new business, Peninsula Pine Landscaping."

Baxter fingered through the charms until he came to the right one. When he held it out,

George grabbed Nancy's arm. Nancy did a double-take when she looked at the charm.

The charm was of a gold pine tree with white-tipped branches that looked like waves. It was identical to the logo on the truck that had nearly run them off the 17-Mile Drive that morning near Joanna Burton's house!

Chapter

Ten

Nancy could hardly believe her eyes. There was a very good chance that she and George had seen Len speeding away from the murder scene.

"Nancy, are you thinking what I'm thinking?" George asked softly.

"Maybe, but let's not jump to any conclusions." Turning to Cy Baxter, she asked, "Do you know if Len has a pickup truck with this logo on the side?"

Baxter nodded.

Okay, slow down, Drew, Nancy cautioned herself. She and George hadn't actually seen Len leave Joanna Burton's house. But she couldn't think of a reason for him to be driving so recklessly—unless he had been up to no good and wanted to get away fast.

Nancy thought back to her encounter with Marcia that morning. If Marcia knew or even suspected that Len had been at Joanna's that morning, that could explain her refusal to answer Nancy's questions.

Nancy knew George was dying to talk this over, but they couldn't in front of Cy Baxter and Rachel.

Nancy was about to say goodbye when Baxter asked, "What about Gigi?" Seeing the girls' perplexed expressions, he added, "Joanna's dog. Who's going to take care of her?"

"The police probably took charge of her. Or maybe Joanna's agent took her home," George said.

"Stephanie Cooke?" Baxter's face turned sour as he mentioned the agent's name. "I can't imagine that she'd go out of her way to help anyone—especially if the person is dead and can't do anything for her. I'd better call the police and check on the dog myself."

Nancy was surprised at Cy Baxter's critical tone. It had seemed to her that the agent was very concerned for her client. "Weren't Joanna and Stephanie close?" Nancy asked.

"Not really. Stephanie's specialty is to take an older actor or actress whose career has fallen off and build it back up." With a quick look at Rachel he added, "I think she represented Michael Davis in his comeback, in fact."

Rachel smiled stiffly and quickly placed the photo of Michael Davis in her drawer. She seemed uncomfortable talking about the actor, but then, why keep his photo on her desk?

After thanking Cy Baxter and Rachel for their time, Nancy and George headed for the door. The clocks in the showroom chimed the hour as they passed through the showroom. Nancy started at the sound. It reminded her of the smashed cuckoo clock that had been delivered to her at the Provence Inn.

A quick glance at the wall of clocks told her that Cy Baxter's cuckoo clock was in the same place it had been the day before. The clock that had been sent to her hadn't come from him—unless Baxter kept a supply of them.

"That's a beautiful cuckoo clock," Nancy commented, pausing to look at it.

Cy Baxter nodded approvingly at the clock. "Isn't it? I have a man in Switzerland who makes them to order for me. That one is just for display," he told her. "Would you like to order one? It takes about four weeks."

"Oh, no—I don't think I could afford one," Nancy said quickly. With a quick goodbye she and George left.

As soon as they were outside, Nancy turned to George and said, "Well, it doesn't look as if Baxter or Rachel sent the clock—unless he was lying about having others there."

"And I don't see how we can get a look at his stockroom," George added. "He keeps a pretty close eye on things."

"He and Rachel both seemed surprised about Joanna Burton's death," Nancy added, her brow furrowed. "My instincts tell me neither of them did it—unless they're very good liars."

"But something funny was going on, don't you think?" George asked. "Rachel was sure acting guilty of *something.*"

"Maybe she's just a nervous person," Nancy said with a shrug. "Come on. Let's go see if Bess got back to the café."

Just before they crossed the street to the restaurant Nancy glanced toward Cheung's Original Designs.

"That's funny. The sign on the door says Closed," Nancy said.

"Why would she close her store in the middle of the day?" George asked, following Nancy's gaze.

Nancy frowned. "I don't know, but I'm definitely going to ask her the next time I see her."

Continuing across the street, Nancy and George crossed into Ted's restaurant. Bess was sitting at a table near the door, eating a chicken salad platter. As soon as she saw Nancy and George, she grinned and waved.

"Did you find out anything about the necklace this morning when you talked to Joanna Burton?" Bess asked. "Okay, what I really want to know is what's she like? And what is her house like?"

Obviously Bess didn't know what had happened to the actress. When Nancy told her, Bess's expression changed to one of horror.

"Oh, no! I had no idea. No wonder Marcia's so upset!" Bess exclaimed.

"You've seen Marcia?" George asked.

Bess nodded. "She and Len came by to ask if we'd accept a delivery because they had to be out of the shop for a while. Come on and sit down. Are you guys hungry?"

Nancy and George shook their heads. "Did Marcia and Len say where they were going?" Nancy asked.

"No," Bess replied. She looked up at Nancy with curious blue eyes. "Why? What's going on?"

Nancy and George quickly filled Bess in on all that had happened that morning. "And we just found out that the truck that nearly ran us off the road is Len's truck. That could tie him to the scene of Joanna Burton's murder," Nancy finished.

"Do you honestly think Len is the one who killed her?" she asked in a whisper. "Maybe Marcia found out, and that's why she acted so weird when you tried to talk to her before."

"Maybe," Nancy said. "We do have to talk to them both." She sighed, then said, "Since they're not around I might as well call the car dealership in Monterey and check out Cy Baxter's alibi."

"Hey, I've got an idea," Bess said brightly. "Let's just drive over there. There's a lot to see in Monterey, and we haven't had a chance to do any sightseeing yet."

George shot a look at the kitchen. "Do you think Ted will let you come with us?" she asked sarcastically.

"What do you mean, *let* me come with you? I'm all finished for the day. Why would he care?" Bess asked. "I even got everything set up for tomorrow so I can take the whole day off."

Nancy asked Bess, "Did Ted mention that we stopped by this morning?"

"No," Bess said. "I wondered where you were."

George glanced briefly around the restaurant before fixing her cousin with a sober gaze. "Bess, did you notice that Ted isn't very excited about us being here? He doesn't seem to like it when you go anyplace with us," she said.

"That's crazy!" Bess said defensively. "He couldn't wait to meet you two."

"Then why does he think of something else for you to do every time we plan to do something together?" George asked.

Bess stabbed a piece of chicken with her fork. "I have a job now, and that job has certain responsibilities. Ted is my boss, George." Bess was starting to sound irritated.

"George didn't mean to put down your job,

Bess," Nancy said quickly. "We're both really glad that you like your work. It's just—"

Nancy broke off as a hand clamped down on her shoulder. Turning around, she saw Stephanie Cooke standing there. The agent was dressed in a white leather jumpsuit studded with sequins. Her red hair was hanging loose down her back in long waves. She seemed to have recovered completely from the morning's disaster.

"I hope you don't mind if I disturb you," Stephanie said. Without waiting for Nancy to answer, she sat down in the only empty chair. "I heard you tell the police detective you were staying at the Provence Inn. The woman at the desk said she thought you might be here."

Leaning forward conspiratorially, Stephanie said in a low voice, "I have a business deal I'd like to discuss with you. It could be very exciting.

"Morgan introduced you as a detective, and I find that so fascinating," Stephanie went on. "I made a few calls to Hollywood."

"Yes?" Nancy prompted, wishing Stephanie would get to the point.

"Anyway, I know some people who are very interested in using some of your stories for films." Stephanie folded her arms across her chest, beaming at Nancy.

"Oh, no," Nancy said quickly. "Something like that could only get in the way of my work."

Stephanie raised an eyebrow. "But, Nancy,

just think of the opportunities this would open up," she said. "You wouldn't have to bother with being a detective any longer."

"Nancy likes what she does, and she's good at it," Bess said indignantly. George nodded her agreement.

"Well, if you're sure you're not interested—"

"Thanks, but no thanks," Nancy said quickly.

Stephanie didn't show any signs of leaving. "What do you think about Joanna?" she asked, changing the subject.

"What do you mean?" George wanted to know.

"Do you have any ideas about what happened to her or to the diamonds?" Stephanie asked.

Why was Stephanie asking *her* this? Nancy wondered. "I really don't know," she answered. "Perhaps you should talk to Detective Bommarito."

Keeping her gaze fixed on Nancy, she said, "Surely you have some theory. Haven't you had a case like this before?" she pressed.

"Every case is different," Nancy said, not wanting to discuss her ideas with Stephanie.

Just then Ted approached the table carrying a tray with three servings of a chocolate dessert on it. "I thought you might like to try Bess's specialty for today, French silk pie."

Now that Bess was there, Ted was acting really nice to Nancy and George. What was his story?

"Um, that looks great, Ted," George said. "Thanks a lot."

Ted smiled at Stephanie. "I'm sorry, I didn't see you sitting here before. Would you like to order something?"

The agent glanced quickly around the table, gauging the others' expressions. To Nancy's relief, she said, "I think my business here is finished." She pointed to an empty table near the jukebox. "I would like to order some lunch, though. Please send a waitress and a menu over there."

Before Stephanie moved to her table she turned to Nancy and said, "Keep my offer in mind, okay? And give me a call if you change your mind."

Bess shook her head, following Stephanie with her eyes. "Wow, she really comes on strong," she whispered.

"I'll say. She sure made a quick comeback from this morning," George added. "She's already making calls trying to put together a movie deal for you, Nancy, right after the death of a supposedly close friend of hers."

"Maybe that's the way she deals with being upset—throwing herself into her work," Ted put in, tucking the empty tray under one arm.

"Maybe," Nancy said. "Or maybe Cy Baxter was right and Stephanie wasn't as good a friend of Joanna Burton's as she claimed." She took a bite of her French silk pie. "Mmm. This is delicious, Bess!"

Bess beamed at the compliment. Turning to Ted, she said, "I'm taking Nancy and George to Monterey this afternoon to have a look around."

Ted immediately frowned.

"I'm all finished with today's baking, and I even have raspberry tarts ready for tomorrow," Bess told him. "There's no reason for me to stay unless you don't think you can put the tarts away when they cool." She grinned up at him flirtatiously.

At first Nancy couldn't read Ted's expression. He seemed to be struggling with some emotion. Then finally he smiled back at Bess and said, "No problem. I can handle that. Have a great time." He bent to kiss Bess on the cheek, then started back toward the kitchen.

The phone at the back of the café rang just as Ted reached the kitchen doors. Stepping over to the extension, he picked up the receiver. He spoke into it briefly, then cupped a hand over the mouthpiece.

"Nancy, it's for you," he called out.

"Maybe it's Marcia," Nancy said hopefully, getting to her feet and hurrying to the phone. "Hello?" she said into the receiver.

"I need to meet with you," said a low, husky voice Nancy didn't recognize. "I have important information about the case you're investigating."

The person sounded nervous, even panicked. "Meet where?" Nancy asked. "Who is this?"

"On the beach, as soon as you can get there," the voice said. "Be sure to come alone."

Nancy racked her brain, trying to think who the caller could be. "How will I know who you are?" she asked.

"I'll know you." There was a click, and the line went dead.

Nancy slowly hung up the phone. Going back to her table, she quickly told Bess and George about the anonymous call. "The voice was disguised," she finished. "I couldn't tell who it was."

"You're not going, are you?" Bess asked, twisting her blond hair nervously in her fingers.

"Of course I'm going."

"Then we're going with you," George said firmly.

Nancy shook her head. "The caller specifically said for me to come alone," she said. "If you guys show up, the person probably won't approach me."

"You don't know what this person has planned for you," Bess objected. "Remember what happened to Joanna Burton," she added grimly.

Despite her friends' objections, Nancy convinced them that she should go alone. As she rose to leave she said, "Okay, so I'll meet you back at the Provence Inn after I'm done. And then we can head to Monterey."

Outside the day had turned foggy and the air was damp and heavy. Nancy walked quickly— she didn't want to risk missing the person who had called.

There were very few people at the beach. The fog must have driven them away, Nancy reasoned. The water was gray, and big waves slammed relentlessly onto the beach.

Nancy quickly made her way down one of the stairways to the hard-packed sand. She began to stroll casually but kept a sharp lookout.

She had gone a few hundred yards when she noticed some large rocks jutting out of the sand. They rose up the sandy hill to the level of the road above, which was edged by a stone wall. "I guess I'll climb up on one and wait there to make contact with the caller," Nancy murmured to herself.

It took only a minute or so to clamber up the rocky incline. When she came to a flat area about halfway up she stopped and sat down. As she looked out at the water she suddenly found herself thinking of Ned. This would be the perfect place to watch the sun set with him, she thought to herself.

The sound of pebbles rolling down from above startled Nancy out of her daydream. She brushed them aside and glanced up at the rocky ledge.

She didn't see anything. Then a loud scraping noise triggered an alarm in her mind. A huge boulder in the wall directly above her was teetering precariously.

Nancy gasped and jumped to her feet. Before she could move away the boulder pulled loose and began rolling down the incline. In a moment it was going to crash right over her!

Chapter

Eleven

First panic gripped Nancy, but then her reflexes took over. She jumped to the side, hoping her feet would find a stable surface to land on.

No sooner did she leave her perch than the boulder crashed down on the very surface where she'd been sitting. It rolled off the opposite side and continued harmlessly down the hill.

"Phew! That was a close—" Nancy then felt loose stones shifting beneath her feet.

"Whoa!" She flung her arms out wildly, trying to maintain her balance, but it was too late. Her feet slipped out from under her, and she slid down the rocks to the beach.

Nancy remained motionless for a few moments, trying to catch her breath. Her whole body ached. There were scratches on her legs, and her jacket was ripped at one elbow. After a while she slowly climbed to her feet.

"Ouch!" She couldn't suppress a groan as a sharp pain shot through her left ankle.

She must have sprained it, she realized. But that wasn't her biggest worry. Something about the way that rock had fallen wasn't right. From what she could see, the rocks in that wall were cemented together. How could one of them have come loose and fallen?

Gritting her teeth, Nancy limped slowly along the sand until she reached the steps leading to the road above. Then she hobbled along the road to the part of the wall where the boulder had fallen. There was no missing the three-foot gap in the wall.

She tested the stones on either side of the gap. The cement around them was crumbling a little, but the stones were basically secure. Nancy was sure they wouldn't fall on their own. Bending closer, she spotted small grooves in the cement surrounding the space where the fallen rock had been. It looked as if something had been used to pry the fallen boulder loose. Someone had purposely pushed the rock toward her!

Nancy felt sick thinking of what might have happened. The person who had called had set her up!

Keeping her weight off her left foot, Nancy peered down at the handful of people on the beach below. Was one of them the caller who had set her up? Nancy didn't see anyone who looked familiar.

By now her ankle was throbbing. She groaned slightly as she started making her way back to the inn. When she got back to her room Bess and George were sitting across from each other on the twin beds.

"Nancy, you're limping!" Bess cried, jumping up and hurrying over to Nancy. "And you're covered with scrapes! What happened?"

Bess helped Nancy to her bed while George ran to the bathroom to get a washcloth.

"I'm sure it looks worse than it is," Nancy assured her friends. "Thanks," she said, taking the washcloth George handed her. While she cleaned up the scratches on her legs she explained what had happened at the beach.

"I don't believe it!" Bess exclaimed, looking outraged. "The person who called wanted to hurt you!"

"And it looks like whoever it was succeeded," George added grimly. She wrapped some ice in a towel and placed it on Nancy's ankle. She gingerly probed the swollen area, causing Nancy to flinch. "I think we'd better take you to the hospital, Nan."

"Are you sure you feel well enough to stop by Marcia's store?" George asked Nancy an hour and a half later.

The two girls were sitting in the front seat of the rental car, which was parked in front of a pharmacy. Bess was inside getting the pain medication that the doctor had prescribed for Nancy's ankle.

"Positive," Nancy assured George. "The doctor said it's only a sprain. I promise I'll rest as soon as we get back to the inn."

George didn't look totally convinced, but she smiled and said, "I guess I should know by now that nothing keeps you off a case once you're hooked. By the way," she said, changing the subject, "I talked to Bess. I'm not sure she's as happy with the idea of moving to Carmel as she's trying to make us believe."

"Really? What makes you say that?" Nancy asked.

George stared out the front windshield. "It wasn't anything specific that she said—it was only hints," she explained. "I got the distinct impression that Ted has rushed her into a decision."

"If she's only staying because Ted is pressuring her to"—Nancy frowned—"there's no way we can let that happen."

"It's *her* decision, though," George said glumly. "I just hope that she decides to do what's best for her—not what's best for Ted."

Bess pulled open the back door of the car. "I got the medication," she announced, handing the small white bag to Nancy. "Let's head back to the inn so you can get some R and R."

"Detective Drew wants to make a pit stop first," George said, flicking a thumb at Nancy. "Marcia Cheung's store." Bess opened her mouth to object, but George cut her off. "I already tried to talk her out of it. No go."

Fifteen minutes later George pulled up in front of the jewelry shop. "The Closed sign is still in the window," she commented.

Nancy frowned. "Let's stop in at the Café de Carmel," she suggested. "Maybe Ted has spoken to Marcia or Len. Besides, we can get something to eat and take it back to the Provence Inn with us."

"Good idea," George agreed. "I don't think you should take that pain medicine on an empty stomach, Nancy."

"I don't see any parking spots," Bess said, scanning the street. "Why don't you two get out here? I'll park the car and meet you, and, Nancy," she added, pointing a warning finger at her, "be sure to keep that ankle up on a chair or something."

"Aye, aye, chief," Nancy said, laughing.

George set the parking brake, and she and Nancy got out while Bess scooted around to the driver's side.

The doctor had taped her ankle, so it didn't hurt too much as Nancy limped across the street and into the Café de Carmel. No sooner did she and George push through the front door than Ted hurried over.

"I've been calling everywhere for you guys!" he said. He looked so worried that all of his earlier moodiness had disappeared.

"Why? What happened?" Nancy wanted to know.

"The police came to the jewelry shop and took Marcia in for questioning about Joanna Burton's murder!" Ted said.

"Oh, no. When did this happen?" Nancy asked. She grimaced as a twinge of pain shot through her ankle. Limping over to the nearest table, she sat down and propped her foot up on another chair.

"They left about an hour ago, not too long after Marcia reopened her store," Ted replied. "She called me because she couldn't find Len. Shouldn't we do something?" he asked.

"Does she have a lawyer?" George asked, taking the seat beside Nancy.

"I don't know. I guess she called one." Ted also sat down momentarily, then looked up suddenly. "Where's Bess?" he asked.

"She's looking for a parking spot," Nancy told him.

Just then the door to the restaurant opened again. Nancy, expecting Bess, was surprised to see Len.

"Does anyone know where Marcia is?" he asked from the doorway.

Ted glanced at Nancy and George before answering. "She's at the police station, being questioned about Joanna Burton's murder," he finally told Len.

Len's mouth fell open. He stepped the rest of the way inside the restaurant, letting the door slam behind him. "How could this happen?" he finally asked. "I have to get down to the station!"

"Wait a minute, Len," Nancy said. She wasn't going to let him leave before he answered a few questions. "I think you have some explaining to do."

"Nancy and I saw you this morning right after you left Joanna Burton's," George added. "We were in that car you almost ran off the road."

"What are you talking about?" Len said. "I wasn't at Joanna Burton's this morning."

"We saw you in your truck, barreling around the curve just beyond Miss Burton's driveway. I almost went over the cliff edge getting out of your way."

Len shook his head. "I've never been to Joanna Burton's house, ever."

He looked so sincere and confused that Nancy almost believed him. Still, she and George had seen him.

"Do you have a pine tree logo painted on the side of your truck—one with branches that look like waves?" George asked impatiently.

Len nodded. "Yeah. So?"

"Were you driving it on the Seventeen-Mile Drive this morning?" Nancy asked.

Len nodded again. He still was looking at Nancy as though she were crazy.

"Well, if you were up there and you *weren't* at Joanna Burton's house, I'd like to know why you were driving like a maniac."

"Stop bothering Len!" a woman's voice spoke up from the doorway of the restaurant.

Marcia Cheung was standing just inside the door, a dark, unreadable expression on her face.

Len hurried to Marcia's side, drawing her close. "Are you all right? What happened?"

Without answering his questions Marcia turned to face the others. "Len wasn't at Joanna Burton's this morning," she said firmly.

"But how can you be sure?" Bess asked hesitantly.

Marcia locked eyes with her fiancé, then replied, "I know because *I* was there."

Chapter

Twelve

NANCY'S MOUTH fell open. "What!" Gazing around the table, she saw that everyone looked as shocked as she felt. "But this morning you said you *weren't* at Joanna Burton's house."

Marcia didn't say anything right away. Pulling up a chair from a neighboring table, she sat down. Len stood behind her with his hands on her shoulders.

Taking a deep breath, Marcia said, "Actually, I wasn't *at* Miss Burton's house. I was just nearby."

"Whoa!" George said, holding up a hand. "I'm totally confused. Maybe you'd better start at the beginning."

"Let me get everyone something to drink," Ted offered. He headed into the kitchen.

Marcia turned her head to look up at Len. "I

guess the story starts with me," he said. "I had an appointment with a client on the Seventeen-Mile Drive this morning."

"Mrs. Kohler lives right next to Joanna Burton," Marcia put in.

"Yeah. So anyway, she told me she wanted an estimate on lawn service," Len went on. "But when I got there, she wanted to talk about her flower beds, too." Len rolled his eyes. "The appointment took much longer than I'd anticipated, and I had another client scheduled at ten."

"Len was rushing to make that second appointment when you saw him." Marcia took over the explanation. She paused as Ted returned with a trayful of glasses filled with iced tea. She took the glass he offered her and sipped it gratefully.

Nancy shot Marcia a questioning look. "But what were *you* doing there?" she asked.

"I was worried about what Len might do." Marcia reached up and put her hand over Len's. "He kept saying that if he could talk to Joanna Burton, he would be able to straighten out the whole diamond mess. I told him to leave everything to you, but Len doesn't always listen.

"This morning we went to our store early, but Len didn't stay long," Marcia said, continuing her story. "He said he had lots of things to do, and he was acting a little agitated. I was afraid he was going to visit Miss Burton, so as soon as he left I decided to follow him."

"This sounds just like a spy movie," Ted

commented, shaking his head. He stood next to Len, his gaze darting to the waitresses every once in a while to make sure they were handling the customers.

Marcia smiled wryly. "I had to stop at the gate to the Seventeen-Mile Drive to pay, and I lost Len for a while. He has a special sticker so he can go on through."

"What kind of sticker?" George interrupted.

"People who go in and out on business can pay a flat fee to get a sticker instead of forking over the regular fee each time. If I had to pay each time I visited a client on the drive, it would run my business costs sky-high," Len explained.

Nancy was dying to hear the rest of the story. "Then what happened?" she urged.

"When I saw Len's truck again, it was parked by the side of the road right by Joanna Burton's house," Marcia explained. "I didn't know what to do. I ended up pulling into a nearby overlook and waiting. I finally got out of the car and started walking toward the house—"

Marcia broke off as the door to the restaurant burst open and Bess came flying in. "I had to park way down the hill," Bess said. "You guys need to do something about the parking around here."

"Bess, sit down and be quiet," Ted said. "Marcia is trying to tell us something."

Bess almost sputtered as she pulled up a chair and sat down between George and Nancy.

"I saw Len next to his truck," Marcia went on. "He couldn't even get the key in the lock, he was so upset. He finally did unlock the door, then he got in and made a U-turn. He drove right by me and didn't even notice."

"Nancy and I must have arrived right after that," George put in, crunching down on an ice cube.

Marcia nodded. "I had just gotten into my car and was about to follow Len when you guys pulled into the overlook. I didn't want to have to answer any questions about why I was there until I talked to Len, so I ducked down in my seat."

"And by the time we left, Len was already out of sight," Nancy guessed. Some of the pieces of this puzzle were starting to fit together, but she wanted to hear the rest of what Marcia had to say.

"That's right," Marcia said. "I decided to go back to the shop to wait for him. Then you came by and told me Joanna was dead. What could I think?" Marcia looked up at Len apologetically.

"I *always* rant and rave when I'm upset," Len said. "It's just the way I let off steam."

Marcia smiled at him. "I guess I should know, but so much was at stake—my whole business."

Turning to Nancy, Marcia said, "That's why I wouldn't talk to you this morning. I had to talk to Len first, and he didn't show up here until after lunch." She let out a nervous laugh. "I'm just glad I talked to him before the police picked me up for questioning. At least I could tell them what really happened. And when the police called, Mrs. Kohler confirmed that Len was there until just before ten o'clock."

Marcia still didn't have proof that *she* had been where she claimed to be, but her story seemed to ring true. Also, Nancy's instincts told her that the same person was probably involved in both crimes. If Len and Marcia hadn't killed Joanna, they probably hadn't stolen her diamonds.

The wheels in Nancy's mind were turning. Assuming that Len and Marcia weren't involved, that left Cy Baxter, his assistant Rachel, and Morgan Fowler as suspects. Cy Baxter had an alibi for the time of Joanna Burton's murder, but Nancy wondered about the other two.

"You must be scaring the person who's responsible," George put in. "Someone shoved that boulder at you this afternoon. And if Marcia was at the police station, it couldn't have been her."

Nancy quickly explained what had happened to the others. "And that's not all. Last night I received a 'gift' of a smashed cuckoo clock with a warning note," she concluded.

"That's awful," Len said. He nodded at Nancy's bandaged ankle. "I was so caught up in what we had to tell you that I didn't even notice that you were hurt. Is it serious?"

He seemed relieved when Nancy told him she'd be okay.

"Nancy needs to get home and rest that ankle, though," Bess said, getting up from her chair. "Let me get us something for dinner first."

"We need to be going, too," Marcia said, standing up.

When Bess returned with a huge paper bag a few minutes later, Ted fixed her with stony dark eyes. "Are you going to be gone all day tomorrow?" he asked her. The annoyance in his voice was clear.

"Ted, you'll do just fine," Bess said simply.

This was the Bess Nancy knew—the one who wouldn't let Ted or any other guy push her around.

Turning back to Nancy, Bess said, "I'll go get the car. I have to go right by a video store on the way, so I think I'll rent a movie, too. We can borrow your VCR, can't we, Ted?" Bess asked.

"Um, sure," Ted said, but his expression told Nancy he wasn't happy about anything.

"I'm going with you to pick out the movie, Bess," George insisted. "I don't want to watch one of those silly romantic things you always rent."

Nancy started to get up, but Bess only shook her head. "Oh, no, you don't. You're not moving an inch until we come back with the car."

"We'll only be a few minutes," George promised. Then she and Bess hurried out of the restaurant.

Ted stared angrily after Bess and George, then stormed back into the kitchen. Nancy was glad, though, that Bess had stuck up for herself.

After a few minutes Nancy got fidgety. "I'll just walk down and find Bess and George," she murmured, getting to her feet.

She tried to ignore the incessant throbbing in her ankle as she left the café and started down Ocean Avenue. Spotting the video store Bess had mentioned about halfway down the block, she limped over to it and peeked in through the window. Bess and George were there, all right— talking to Morgan Fowler!

Great, Nancy thought. This was a chance to find out more about what he knew about the diamond theft and Joanna Burton's murder.

"What are you doing here?" Bess asked as Nancy joined them. "You shouldn't be walking."

"I wanted to help you pick out a movie," said Nancy. "Hi, Morgan."

The actor smiled a hello. "I'm surprised to see you up and around after your fall this afternoon," he said. "But it looks like your friends picked out a good movie for you," he said.

George held up a videocassette. On the cover was a young woman peering through a magnifying glass. The title of the movie was *Diamond Deceit,* and the woman on the cover, Joanna Burton. She was playing Trish Tottenham, a detective.

"I go for action-adventure movies myself,"

Morgan said, holding up a box with a warrior dressed in space-age fighting gear.

As the group headed for the counter, Bess said, "Morgan has some great news," she said. "He got a part in a movie!"

Morgan turned to Nancy, flashing her one of his winning smiles. "I just quit Seaside Security. Stephanie Cooke thinks she has a part for me in a movie, *and* she's agreed to be my agent."

"That *is* good news," Nancy said, but her mind wasn't really on what he was telling her. She was trying to think of a way to turn the conversation to the case.

Morgan paid the girl at the counter for his movie, then turned back to Nancy. "Stephanie was involved in a big comeback deal for Joanna," he said. "That's the movie she has in mind for me. You know Michael Davis?" When Nancy nodded, he continued. "Stephanie thinks she can get Joanna's movie rewritten for a male lead. Michael Davis is one of her clients. If he agrees to do the movie, she thinks there's a part in it for me," Morgan finished with a proud smile.

He waved his videocassette at Nancy, Bess, and George. "Well, see you later." Before Nancy could think about how to turn the conversation to the missing diamonds, he was gone.

"This ankle must be making me lightheaded," she muttered to herself.

"Your ankle hurts?" Bess asked worriedly.

"We'd better get you back to the inn," George

added, stepping away from the counter with their videocassette.

Bess gave Nancy a stern look. "You wait here, and I'll go get the car," she said.

The three of them walked out of the shop together. Spotting a bench a short way down the hill, Nancy went to it and sat. George stopped in a newsstand next to the video store and picked up a paper.

"This will give us something to read while we wait for Bess," George said, joining Nancy at the bench.

George pulled out the sports section of the newspaper and handed the rest to Nancy. Nancy immediately scanned the headlines.

"Police Seek Clues in Death of Movie Queen," the headline read. "George, here's a story about Joanna Burton." Nancy held out the paper so they could both read the article.

The story didn't give many details, saying only that the actress's body had been found on the beach behind her house, and that foul play was suspected. Most of the article focused on Joanna Burton's film career.

"It says she was going to do another Trish Tottenham movie, a mature Trish," George said. "That must be the movie Morgan was talking about. He may be getting his hopes up a little soon, though." George pointed to a part of the story Nancy hadn't read yet. "It says that the future of the picture is in doubt because Joanna was providing a portion of the financing."

Nancy sat up straight. That didn't make sense. "She didn't have any money of her own. Cy Baxter said she didn't pay her bills, and we saw how worn her house was. Where would she get the money to invest in a movie?"

In a flash the solution suddenly became clear to Nancy. "Unless she planned on coming into some big money soon—money from the sale of some diamonds!"

"What are you talking about?" George asked, crinkling up her nose.

Nancy sat forward excitedly. "George, I have a feeling that the person who stole Joanna Burton's diamonds was Joanna herself!"

Chapter

Thirteen

GEORGE WAS STARING at Nancy as if she'd lost her mind. "Will you please speak English?" she said. "Nothing you just said makes sense."

"Okay. Let's say Joanna Burton replaced the diamonds with cubic zirconia herself," Nancy began. "Then she pretended that someone else made the switch so she could collect on her insurance for the missing diamonds."

Understanding lit up George's brown eyes. "That *would* be an ideal way for her to raise money," she agreed. "Then she'd have the insurance money *and* the diamonds, in case she needed to sell them to raise more money."

Nancy frowned as another thought occurred to her. "Wait a minute. If Joanna Burton did steal her own diamonds, then who killed her? And why?"

"Maybe she caught someone trying to take the diamonds from her, and that person got scared and killed her," George suggested, shrugging.

"That makes sense," Nancy agreed. "Or maybe the guilty person is someone who might profit from her death. I don't see what reason Cy Baxter would have, or his assistant. Joanna Burton's agent, Stephanie, would only lose money if she murdered the actress."

Nancy paused, snapping her fingers. "The only person who's come out ahead in this scheme is Morgan Fowler. He has a role in a movie and a new agent!"

Bess pulled the car up to the curb and honked. After climbing in, Nancy and George quickly filled Bess in on what they had been discussing.

"What?" Bess exclaimed, her mouth hanging open. "Do you really think she'd steal her own diamonds and let someone else take the blame?"

"Maybe if she wanted to make a film comeback badly enough," Nancy answered. "I wish I could go out to Joanna Burton's house and look around, but I'm sure the police have it sealed off. Maybe I could find something out there to help me figure this out."

"Like the diamonds?" Bess asked.

Nancy nodded. "Or some clue as to who Miss Burton's killer was."

Within minutes the girls had arrived at the Provence Inn. As soon as they got to Nancy and

George's room Bess went for Ted's videocassette recorder, and George unpacked their dinner.

"Don't think about doing anything but resting tonight," Bess told Nancy. "You're getting into bed and staying there."

Nancy didn't protest. Her ankle was throbbing painfully, and she didn't think she could have made it to Joanna Burton's house even if there was a way for her to get in. When Bess brought her two of her pills for pain, Nancy took them gratefully.

"Let's eat and watch the movie at the same time," Bess suggested, slipping the videocassette into the VCR.

When Bess turned off the lights, Nancy set her half-eaten roast beef sandwich aside and tried to get comfortable. She wasn't sure she'd seen this movie before. It opened with Trish attending a formal dinner. There were lots of people Nancy knew she should be able to name but couldn't. About halfway through the dinner one of the guests discovered that her diamond ring was missing.

Nancy blinked, trying to stay awake. "Boy, this medicine is really making me sleepy," she murmured.

"Mmm," Bess said vaguely, her attention focused on the screen.

Nancy's lids were growing heavier and heavier. She decided to rest her eyes for just a minute.

* * *

In the back of her mind Nancy heard a squeaking noise she couldn't quite identify. "Hmm—what—"

She cracked open an eye, trying to figure out what was making the noise, then came fully awake when she saw daylight streaming in the window.

"Wow, it's morning," she said, sitting up. She was still wearing her clothes, but someone had covered her with a blanket. The noise she'd heard was George turning off the shower.

A moment later George came out of the bathroom, wearing a bathrobe and drying her short, dark hair with a towel. "Good morning, sleepyhead," she greeted Nancy cheerfully.

"What time is it?" Nancy asked.

"Almost nine o'clock. You slept for hours," George told her.

"I feel so lazy." Nancy stretched. "Once I took that medicine, I just couldn't stay awake."

"How's your ankle this morning?" George asked.

Nancy gingerly moved her left foot, rotating it in a circle. It felt stiff, but not nearly so painful as it had the night before. Swinging her legs over the side of the bed, she gingerly put her weight on her left leg.

"It still hurts, but not much," she announced.

The telephone rang just then, and Nancy reached out to answer it. "Hi, Mr. Menendez," she said. "I'm fine. Really."

Nancy laughed. "I don't think I'm ready for golf," she said, and she noticed George's face light up. "But George might want to go. Here, I'll put her on."

George shook her head and backed away. "I'm not going to leave you here alone," she whispered.

Nancy covered the mouthpiece with her hand. "That's silly. You love golf, and this is your chance to play."

She held the phone out again, and this time George took it. "You're sure? What will you do?" she asked Nancy.

Nancy nodded. "Right now I'm going to take a long, hot shower. I'll be fine," she assured George.

While George spoke to Mr. Menendez, Nancy grabbed some fresh clothes and stepped into the small, steamy bathroom.

"Bess is here with breakfast," George yelled just as Nancy finished dressing and rewrapping her ankle with the Ace bandage.

"How'd the movie turn out last night?" she asked as she joined Bess and George at the small table set up in the kitchenette.

"Trish Tottenham solved the mystery and caught the bad guys," Bess said with a grin. "As usual."

George finished up her apple muffin, then stood up. "Sorry to eat and run, but I've got to meet Mr. Menendez in the lobby in about two minutes," she said. "Leave a note if you guys go anywhere, okay?" With a quick wave she grabbed her golf clubs and left.

"So what should we do today?" Nancy asked, smiling at Bess. "I'm glad you've got the day off."

Getting up from the table, Bess went over to Nancy's bed and flopped down on it. "I think I need a break from that place."

"The restaurant?" Nancy asked. "I thought you loved it there."

"I do—I mean, I did." She sighed, tugging at the hem of the open-weave sweater she wore over her red tank top and bicycle shorts. "It's not the work that's getting to me. And I really like Ted, too. It's just that, well—he gets pretty jealous when you guys are around. It's kind of hard on me."

Nancy wasn't sure of what to say. "He does seem kind of possessive about you," she finally ventured.

"He doesn't mean anything by it," Bess hurried to add. "But—"

She broke off as the phone rang. Reaching over, Bess picked up the receiver and said, "Hello? Hi, Ted."

Nancy sipped on a glass of orange juice and poured milk over her cereal.

"You promised me you'd put those tarts away so they wouldn't spoil," Bess said into the receiver angrily.

Nancy saw Bess's face turn red. "Nancy and

George have been here two days, and we haven't done any of the things I'd planned. Can't you order something from one of the bakeries? Oh, okay, I guess I could do that," Bess said reluctantly. Then she slammed the receiver down.

"I can't believe it," she told Nancy. "I asked Ted to do one simple thing—put the pastries in the refrigerator when he closed up last night. Well, he forgot, and they spoiled. So I have to go make something to serve today."

Nancy felt awful for her friend. Bess was obviously upset that their day together was being interrupted. "Did he say why he couldn't get desserts from someplace else?" Nancy asked.

"He said some people are coming just to try my desserts," she said.

Nancy frowned. She wouldn't be surprised if Ted had lied. Then, smiling at Bess, she managed to say, "Go on and make the desserts. You can probably be done before George gets back. Then we can all do something together this afternoon. It will do me good to rest my ankle a little longer."

Bess came over and gave Nancy a hug. "Thanks for being so understanding. What will you do all morning?"

"I think I might watch the end of the Trish Tottenham movie," Nancy said.

"Good idea. I'll set it up." Bess went over to the TV and turned it on. "Tell me when you want me to stop."

Nancy moved over to the bed, carrying her juice. She watched the high-speed action on the screen until she saw a scene she didn't remember. "Stop," she said.

"Call me at the restaurant if you need anything," Bess said, and then she left.

Settling back on her bed, Nancy turned her attention to what was happening on screen. In the movie, Joanna Burton in her Trish Tottenham role was searching for a stolen diamond. Nancy wasn't exactly clear as to who had taken the gem, but Trish seemed to know exactly whom she was after. Trish carefully searched a house as music played to a crescendo in the background. When she found the diamond, Nancy was struck by the simplicity of the hiding place.

"I don't believe it!" she exclaimed, staring at the screen. "I know where Joanna Burton hid her diamonds! I've got to get out to her house now!"

Nancy stood up, ignoring the slight twinge of pain in her ankle. She grimaced as she slipped her swollen left foot into her sneaker, but she finally managed to get it on, leaving the laces very loosely tied.

Nancy scribbled a quick note to Bess and George telling them where she was going. Then she grabbed her purse and rummaged for the keys to the rental car.

She limped out to the car. As she unlocked the door, Nancy heard furtive footsteps approaching her from behind. Fear shot through her. Nancy whirled around and found herself face-to-face with Cy Baxter's assistant.

"Rachel!" Nancy exclaimed, fighting down her fear. "What are you doing here?"

On second glance Nancy saw that Rachel was as frightened as she'd been. She was still wearing the navy dress she'd had on the day before. Her dark hair was a mess, and she wore no makeup.

"You've got to help me," Rachel pleaded, grabbing Nancy's arm. "My life is in grave danger."

Chapter

Fourteen

"WHAT ARE YOU talking about?" Nancy asked. "How did you find me here?"

Rachel kept her hand on Nancy's arm. "I got the address from the guest register at Baxter's Fine Jewelry," she said. "Please, you have to help me!"

"Shouldn't you talk to the police if your life is in danger?"

"You don't understand. I can't go to the police. Besides, if it weren't for you, I wouldn't even know I was in any danger," Rachel said. Her eyes flitted around nervously as if she were afraid someone would pop out of the parking lot to attack her.

Nancy stared at the jeweler's assistant, totally puzzled. "If it weren't for me," she echoed. "Why don't you start at the beginning and tell me why you think you're in danger?" Nancy suggested.

Rachel took a deep breath before beginning. "I'm the one who replaced the diamonds in Joanna Burton's necklace with cubic zirconia," she confessed.

"You?" Nancy said, startled.

Rachel nodded. "I knew it was wrong from the first, but I had to do it." Her eyes started tearing up, and she wiped at them with the back of one hand before continuing.

"I used to work for Grand Central Studios in Hollywood, in the wardrobe department. It was so exciting, and I got to meet all the stars. One of my favorites was Michael Davis. I idolized him.

"I worked on a movie he was starring in, and one day when I was getting the costumes from his dressing room, I found a fake sapphire ring that Mr. Davis had worn in the movie. They'd finished shooting that day, so I thought no one would miss it. I picked it up and stuck it in my pocket."

Nancy didn't see what any of this had to do with Joanna Burton's death or the stolen diamonds, but she listened patiently. "When was that?" she asked.

"About three years ago, just as he was making his comeback," Rachel replied. "Anyway, it turned out that the ring wasn't an imitation. The sapphire was real and worth a lot of money, and the ring belonged to Michael!" Rachel's eyes widened. "Was there ever an uproar on the set when he found out it was missing!"

Rachel pushed her hair out of her face, then took a deep breath. "I was afraid to admit I'd taken the ring, so I decided to sneak it back into his dressing room. Wouldn't you know his agent walked in and caught me with it?"

"His agent?" Nancy echoed.

"Stephanie Cooke," Rachel said, nodding. "She saw me with the ring. I tried to explain, and she was very nice about it. I put the ring back, but the next day I was fired. No one mentioned the ring, but I knew that Stephanie had something to do with it. That was when I moved here."

Nancy felt sorry for Rachel, but she still wasn't sure what the point of the story was. "What does all that have to do with Joanna Burton or the necklace or me?" Nancy asked.

"I'm getting to that part," Rachel said, holding up a hand. "I moved to Carmel and got a job with Mr. Baxter. He's been teaching me how to work on jewelry. One day Stephanie came into the shop with Miss Burton. I hoped that she wouldn't recognize me, but she did. A few weeks later she called me."

Tears began to run down Rachel's cheeks. Nancy opened her purse and handed Rachel a tissue.

"She said she had a job for me," Rachel continued, wiping her eyes. "Miss Burton had a diamond necklace she wanted to wear, but it was so valuable she didn't want to wear it in public. She hadn't yet had time to get an imitation of it made, so she wanted to know if I would take out the real stones and reset the necklace with fakes."

Nancy was beginning to see where this story was going. "And?" she prompted.

"I didn't want to do it, but when I hesitated, Stephanie reminded me that Mr. Baxter probably didn't know about my tendency to take things that didn't belong to me."

So Stephanie had been in on the insurance scam with Joanna, Nancy now knew. Still, Stephanie must not know where the real diamonds were hidden. If she did, she would never have asked Nancy about *her* theories of where the gems might be.

"Stephanie brought me the paste, the fake stones, that had been in Joanna Burton's old necklace," Rachel continued. "She told me to take the real diamonds out of the new necklace and replace them with the fakes."

"Is that the way it's usually done?" Nancy asked.

Rachel shook her head. "Usually the paste and the original are two separate pieces. I'd never heard of taking apart an original and making it a fake," Rachel said. "But I didn't feel that I had much choice in the matter. I like it here in Carmel. I'm trying to stick it out with Mr. Baxter until I learn enough."

"So you replaced the diamonds with the fake

stones," Nancy said. That explained why there were scratches on the necklace—Rachel wasn't very experienced as a jeweler. "Didn't you wonder why you were asked to do it?"

"Of course," Rachel replied, "but with Stephanie threatening me, I figured it would be better not to ask. I did all the work when Mr. Baxter wasn't there. He wouldn't have liked me doing work without its going through him first." She shook her head and added, "I must have been out of the store when Miss Burton brought the necklace in to have Mr. Baxter appraise it. I didn't know he had found the fakes until you and your friends came in pretending to be customers."

"Why didn't you go to the police then?" Nancy wanted to know.

Rachel glanced nervously over her shoulder. "Stephanie called me from L.A. on Thursday night. I was still in shock about the whole thing then and hadn't decided what to do. She told me that you were investigating the gem switch. She said that if I told anyone about my part in it, she'd make it look as if I was behind the whole scam."

Suddenly another piece of the puzzle fell into place for Nancy. "So that's when you sent me that smashed cuckoo clock, to try to scare me off the case."

A blush came to Rachel's cheeks as she nodded. "After I heard about Miss Burton's death, I was scared. That clock had just come in for a customer, but I sent it to you instead. Cy will kill me when he finds out.

"And when I saw that picture of Michael Davis yesterday, I really panicked. It's not mine. I know Stephanie left it for me as a threat. That's when I decided to talk to you and tell you the truth. I guess I was hoping you could help me decide what to do. I called you first at the inn. The woman there said to try the Café de Carmel. When I got down by the beach I saw a big rock tumbling down toward you. I knew it wasn't an accident because I saw someone running away."

"You saw the person?" Nancy asked, grabbing Rachel's arm. "Who was it?"

"I wasn't close enough to tell, but I think it was a man. Anyway, I got out of there as fast as I could. I've been driving around in my car all night, too afraid to even go home. What if someone's waiting for me there?" Rachel said in a voice edged with panic.

A man, thought Nancy. Morgan Fowler? He seemed to be around when anything was happening in the case. Nancy recalled his sudden appearance outside Marcia's store and the way he had popped up in the video store.

Now that she thought about it, there was something else suspicious about him. He'd asked about her fall from the rocks. How could he have known about that unless he was there? Nancy hadn't had the impression that Bess or George had told him—she'd have to check with her friends.

Nancy tore herself from her thoughts. Giving the jeweler's assistant an encouraging smile, Nancy said, "Rachel, it's important that you go to the police with this information. From what you've told me, I don't think you've done anything really wrong. And the police will definitely go easier on you if you cooperate with them. Your information will probably help them catch Joanna Burton's killer."

Rachel hesitated only a moment before saying, "I guess I should. Will you go with me?"

Nancy was torn. She hated to leave Rachel alone, but she simply couldn't wait any longer to search Joanna Burton's house. "There's something I *must* do now. Why don't we meet back here?" Nancy looked at her watch. "At noon."

Rachel reluctantly agreed. Finally Nancy was able to get into her car and leave.

As she drove, something Rachel had told her came back to Nancy. Rachel had said that Stephanie called her on Thursday night *from Los Angeles*. The drive to Carmel from L.A. had to be five or six hours long. Stephanie must have gotten up awfully early on Friday to arrive at ten A.M.—unless she had lied about when she arrived in Carmel. Nancy recalled the two coffee cups on Joanna Burton's terrace. Could Stephanie Cooke have been the actress's visitor? Also, how did Stephanie know Nancy was investigating?

Joanna Burton didn't know. Someone else must have told her. Another accomplice? A third person involved?

Nancy hoped to find some clues at Joanna Burton's. She drove to the overlook near the actress's house without any idea of how she was going to get inside the fence. Climbing over it with her sprained ankle would be impossible.

When Nancy got to the black iron gates, she was amazed to see that one of them was slightly ajar. Had the police been so careless as to forget to check it?

Nancy slipped through the narrow opening. As she walked down the drive she spotted the yellow police tape across the front door.

"What's this?" she murmured to herself. The garage doors were open!

Nancy's hair stood on end. Were the police there again? She didn't see any patrol cars. Peeking inside the garage, Nancy did a double-take. Stephanie Cooke's silver sports car was parked inside.

Of course! The agent was probably there searching for the diamonds!

Nancy darted forward and pressed her face against the car window. Immediately she spied a gold charm bracelet lying in the change bin between the two front seats. The bracelet was spread out, and it was easy to see there was a gap between two charms.

Nancy quickly took in the other charms—a lone cypress, a spouting whale, and several others. But there was no sea otter. Nancy let out a low whistle. So Stephanie had pushed Joanna Burton down the balcony stairs!

Nancy's mind raced, trying to fit together all the pieces of the case. Chances were that Stephanie was the person who'd been drinking coffee with Joanna Burton. That meant the agent had come up from L.A. earlier than she claimed.

Still, Nancy couldn't understand why Stephanie would kill Joanna when they were on the brink of closing a big deal. There was one person who could answer Nancy's questions, but Nancy had the feeling Stephanie wouldn't be cooperative.

"I can't leave without testing my theory about where the diamonds are," Nancy whispered out loud.

The police seal on the door leading from the garage to the house was already broken, Nancy saw. Stephanie was probably still inside. If Nancy could sneak in undetected, she could call the police from inside *and* look for the diamonds.

Nancy held her breath, trying the doorknob. It turned easily. Slipping inside, she paused to listen. The only noise she heard was that of her own pounding heart.

She tiptoed down a long hall to the kitchen, which was just off the living room. Nancy immediately spied a telephone hanging on the wall near the sink. She started toward it, then went to the refrigerator instead.

She closed her eyes for a moment, picturing Trish Tottenham's search for the diamond in *Diamond Deceit*. Nancy opened the freezer door and took out the single tray of ice, just as she'd watched Trish Tottenham do.

Carrying the tray to the sink, she turned on a thin stream of hot water and held the tray beneath it. She watched as the cubes slowly melted.

"Wow!" Nancy exclaimed softly. Her eyes opened wide as she stared down at a tray studded with a dozen sparkling diamonds.

Chapter

Fifteen

NANCY'S HEART was pounding as she carefully scooped the diamonds out of the tray. She could hardly believe it—she had found the gems! Joanna Burton had hidden them in the exact same place as the detective she had portrayed in the movie.

Keeping the diamonds carefully grasped in her hand, Nancy hurried to the kitchen phone. As soon as she lifted the receiver she heard Stephanie's voice on the line.

"I tried everywhere, but—" The agent broke off suddenly. "Someone's in the house. They picked up an extension," Nancy heard Stephanie say.

"You know what to do," a man's voice responded. It was Morgan Fowler! So there *was* another accomplice.

Adrenaline shot through Nancy as she realized she'd been found out. She slammed the phone down and searched frantically for the nearest way out. She headed for the terrace doors she and George had used the day before and frantically pulled on the doorknobs. They were locked.

She was just opening the lock when Stephanie's icy voice spoke up from behind her. "Ms. Drew, how nice of you to drop by!"

Nancy turned around slowly, holding the diamonds behind her. As inconspicuously as possible she eased the stones into the back pocket of her jeans. She didn't like the way Stephanie was looking at her—as if she were a trapped mouse.

"Have you finished your little investigation yet?" the agent asked pleasantly.

Nancy knew what Stephanie was getting at. She wanted to know if Nancy had found the diamonds.

"I was hoping that maybe I'd run across the diamonds," Nancy replied just as pleasantly.

"Don't waste your time. I've scoured this place from top to bottom. They aren't here." Stephanie eyed Nancy slyly. "Where were you thinking of looking?"

Nancy shrugged. "No place in particular."

"Come on, Nancy. You're a better detective than that."

"I'm good enough to have figured out your little scheme," Nancy said, stalling. With Bess at the restaurant and George playing golf, it could be hours before they got the note saying where Nancy had gone!

"Is that right? Do tell," the agent said sarcastically.

"The reason the diamonds were replaced with fakes was to get insurance money to finance the movie that would give Joanna Burton her big comeback break," Nancy began.

"Very good," Stephanie said, impressed. "The only way Joanna could get a part was to buy her way in. Since she didn't have any money, I convinced her that we could sell her jewelry. The sentimental old fool didn't want to get rid of the diamonds her dear, departed husband had given her. I had to figure out a way we could get the money and still keep the diamonds. Not a bad plan, eh?" Stephanie said proudly.

"What I can't understand is why you murdered her," Nancy said.

For a brief moment Stephanie's eyes showed a flicker of sadness. "That wasn't part of the plan," she said quickly. "Joanna was going to back out of the scam when she heard that Marcia might be arrested for theft. She said she didn't realize that someone else might be hurt. Even though it was the middle of the night, I got in my car and drove up from L.A. I didn't get here until after two in the morning. I tried all night to talk some sense into her. I told her I'd take care of it, but she fired me!"

"So you pushed her?" Nancy guessed, keeping her voice calm.

"I didn't mean to," Stephanie said, "but I was tired and angry. As Joanna was walking away from me, I took her by the shoulders and tried to shake some sense into her." Stephanie pointed out the French doors. "She was standing there at the top of the steps."

The agent's voice took on a faraway tone. Nancy could tell that she was reliving the awful moment. "When I let go, Joanna swayed for a moment. I reached out to try to catch her," Stephanie went on, her voice rising. "I caught hold of her beach wrap, but the seam tore. She grabbed at my arm but missed and tumbled down the steps."

"Then what happened?" Nancy asked gently.

Stephanie's eyes flitted wildly around the room. "I—I panicked. I ran out to my car and drove away. Then I remembered that the diamonds were still in the house. I wanted those stones. I turned around and drove back, but you were already here."

Nancy felt fear rise as Stephanie glared at her. While the agent was talking, Nancy stood with her back to the terrace doors. With her hand behind her back she was trying to find the catch to unlock the doors. She knew she had to keep Stephanie's attention focused elsewhere until she had the lock open.

"What about your new client, Morgan Fowler? What does he have to do with this?" Nancy asked.

"Morgan. I'll use part of the money from the sale of the diamonds to help his movie career. He's shown me just how loyal and helpful he can be," Stephanie said.

Suddenly the last pieces of the puzzle fell into place. "He must have left that picture for Rachel. He could have sneaked in there. And he must have pushed that rock at me on the beach yesterday."

"Right again," Stephanie said, smiling. She didn't seem at all nervous that Nancy had pieced it all together. "He's wanted to make it as an actor for so long. He knows I can help him, so he's willing to do almost anything for me."

"You certainly had me fooled. You practically ignored him when you arrived here yesterday," Nancy said, still trying to turn the lock.

"I couldn't have people thinking that I had time for an unknown like him," Stephanie said.

"He must have given you the security code to Miss Burton's gate so you could get in today," Nancy said.

Stephanie nodded. She tapped her lips with one finger, studying Nancy. "What am I going to do with you?"

Nancy took a quick breath. She didn't know how much longer she could distract Stephanie.

"Rachel is at the police station right now, telling them everything she knows," Nancy lied. She had to try anything.

"That's a laugh!" Stephanie said. "The police will end up putting her in jail once Morgan and I are through with her."

Nancy shot the agent a nervous glance. "Why? What have you done?"

"It's what we're *going* to do that's important," Stephanie said. "Rachel will be the one who gets blamed for the diamond theft, Joanna's murder —everything. You see, the police will find out that she has a history of stealing jewels that don't belong to her. They'll find the old setting for Joanna's diamonds hidden in Rachel's apartment. Morgan will find a good spot for it. I'm sure the police will assume she killed Joanna, too."

"I'm sure," Nancy said sarcastically.

"But enough about Rachel," Stephanie said, her expression hardening.

As the agent started toward her, Nancy knew her time was up. She twisted the lock one last time, and it turned!

Stephanie slipped in a small puddle of water left by the dripping diamonds. Nancy didn't waste a second. Yanking open the terrace doors, she tore outside.

She tried to run but was slowed by the pain in her ankle. The stairs leading to the beach were right in front of her, and Nancy started down them.

She gasped when she felt hands shove against her back. She swayed slightly, then plunged forward.

"No!" Nancy screamed. The last thing she felt was a blinding pain as her head struck the stairs. Then everything went black.

Chapter

Sixteen

NANCY COULDN'T figure out why she had her clothes on in the bathtub or why she'd let the water get so cold. She didn't want to open her eyes to find out, because her head was throbbing.

At last she managed to open one eye, but all she saw was swirling gray. Perhaps her dream wasn't over yet. Nancy opened both eyes, then slowly sat up. If she was dreaming, her head and ankle wouldn't hurt so much.

Beneath her Nancy felt the rough surface of a large rock. Water lapped gently against her body, and fog wrapped her in a gray blanket. She couldn't see more than two feet in front of her.

Nancy tried to think where she was. How had she ended up here?

Then it all came back to her—the scene with Stephanie and getting pushed down the steps.

She gingerly felt her forehead, flinching as she touched the bump there.

Just then a wave swept over Nancy, drenching her. She felt its powerful pull. The tide was coming in. Nancy's heart leapt into her throat as she realized that Stephanie must have dragged her onto a rock offshore and left her to drown! The water was already up to her chin. Soon it would cover her completely.

"The diamonds!" Nancy gasped aloud. Her hand moved automatically to her back pocket. It was empty. Stephanie had gotten them!

Nancy let out a frustrated groan. How was she going to get out of there? She dangled her foot, then her leg, off the rock but couldn't find solid ground. The water was too deep. She searched for the shoreline, but all she saw was a constant and steady gray mist.

"Help!" Nancy shouted with all the strength she could muster. There was no response. She yelled again, even though it made her head hurt more.

How long have I been unconscious? She wondered. Despite her throbbing ankle, Nancy stood up—the water was too high to sit anymore. Waves continued to wash over the rock, each one higher than the last.

"How am I going to get out of this one?" she wondered out loud. She could swim, but if she chose the wrong direction, she'd be a goner.

"Hey, wait a minute," Nancy murmured as

another wave crashed over her. Waves moved *toward* the beach, didn't they? All she had to do was swim with the flow of water.

Nancy lowered herself into the water and waited for the next wave. As it came toward her she kicked along with it. The pain in her ankle and her head made her feel faint, but she forced herself to keep moving. "Come on, Drew," she urged.

She didn't know how long she swam, but just when she thought she couldn't last another second her feet touched the sandy bottom. Nancy crawled out of the water and collapsed on the beach, shivering.

Too exhausted to move, she drew in huge, gulping breaths of air. When she finally caught her breath, she slowly got to her feet. She had to call the police!

Nancy cocked her head to one side, listening. Was that someone calling her name? She listened again, then grinned.

"Over here! Bess, George, I'm over here!" she called back.

Out of the fog her two friends appeared, both of them worried.

"How did you find me?" Nancy asked as the two girls hugged her, then wrapped her in a blanket George was carrying.

"It wasn't easy," George said. "I read your note when I got back from my golf game around lunchtime. It seemed to be taking you a long time to get back, so I called Bess, and we came out here pronto."

Bess picked up the story. "When we got here, police were everywhere. Seaside Security called them because they found the front gate open when they were making their rounds. But there was no sign of you."

"Stephanie opened the gate," Nancy said, wrapping the blanket more tightly around her.

"Stephanie?" George looked surprised. "She said it was open when she arrived, and that you hadn't ever been here. We knew you had because we saw the car parked at the overlook. She insisted it wouldn't do any good to look for you here. Boy, am I glad we didn't listen to her."

"Where is Stephanie now?" Nancy asked. "She hasn't gotten away yet, has she?"

"Gotten away? What are you talking about?" George asked, perplexed.

A horrified shiver ran through Nancy. "You mean the police didn't find out?" Nancy started to move down the beach, propelled by a new sense of urgency. "I don't have time to go into it now, but Stephanie has the diamonds, and she killed Joanna. We have to stop her!"

"But Stephanie said that Cy Baxter's assistant, Rachel, made the switch," Bess said. She caught up with Nancy, supporting her with one arm.

Nancy shook her head. "Stephanie and Morgan are framing Rachel."

"Uh-oh," George said, frowning. "Morgan is

with Stephanie at Joanna Burton's house right now! Stephanie said that she wanted to get some of her belongings at the house. But, Nancy, the house is back the other way."

Nancy frowned down at her swollen ankle. "George, you can run faster than I can. Go on ahead and make sure Stephanie doesn't get away."

"You got it!" George sprinted and was soon swallowed up by the fog.

Nancy and Bess followed behind as quickly as they could. When they reached the steps leading to Joanna Burton's terrace, Nancy ran up them. Bad ankle or no, she couldn't lose a second! She raced across the terrace, threw open the doors, and hurried inside the house. She heard Bess behind her.

"You let go of me this instant!" Stephanie was yelling at the front door. Hurrying over, Nancy saw that George had the agent in an arm lock. The agent was clutching a small bag in one hand.

"You have no right!" Stephanie continued ranting. "I'm calling my lawyer—"

The agent broke off when her gaze fell on Nancy. Stephanie's face went completely white.

Nancy was relieved to see Detective Bommarito come down the stairs from the second floor, accompanied by Morgan Fowler. "What's going on here?" the detective asked, staring at Nancy's sopping wet clothes. "What happened to you?"

"I'll be glad to tell you everything," Nancy said. "But first I think you should search these two." She nodded toward Stephanie and Morgan. "One of them has Joanna Burton's diamonds."

Nancy lay back in her bed at the Provence Inn, her ankle propped up on pillows and wrapped in an ice pack. "Come on in," she said, motioning to the three people standing in the doorway.

"Are you sure you feel up to it?" Marcia asked. Len and Ted crowded in behind her.

"I do if you've brought food. I'm starving!" Nancy said, grinning.

Bess held the door open. Ted set a platter of fruit on the table beside Nancy's bed. Nancy immediately took an apple slice.

After moving over beside Nancy's bed, Marcia stood and twisted her bracelet. "How can we ever thank you?" she asked.

"You don't have to," Nancy told her. She watched out of the corner of her eye as Ted pulled Bess aside and spoke quietly to her. Bess said something to him, then they slipped out the door.

Finally Len cleared his throat and said, "Business is great now that people know we didn't steal Joanna Burton's diamonds. I can't believe how many calls Marcia and I both have had since our names appeared in the newspaper."

"I'm really glad for you," George said.

Marcia held out a charm for George and

Nancy to see. "Look, Len gave me this. It's the logo for his landscaping business. Isn't it darling?"

"It's beautiful," Nancy said, acting as if she'd never seen the charm before. She picked up a jeweler's box from the bedside table and opened it, showing Marcia and Len a charm bracelet with a sea otter hanging from it. "Bess and George and I got bracelets, too."

George held out her arm, decorated with the same bracelet. "They're from Rachel. She was so grateful that we cleared her name and found the real culprits that she sent these over as gifts."

Marcia smiled, then looked at Len. "We're not going to stay. We just wanted to know if you'd come back in October for our wedding."

"I'd love to come," Nancy said right away. She was really happy that things had worked out for Marcia and Len.

Marcia gave Nancy a hug, then she and Len left.

"Romance is definitely in the air," Nancy said after the door closed. "Speaking of which, I wonder where Bess and Ted went."

"Who knows? A romantic walk on the beach?" George said. "I guess we'll have to get used to the idea that Bess is moving here."

Nancy forced a smile. "If she's happy, then we should be happy for her," she said.

George handed Nancy another slice of apple and picked up a banana for herself. She sat down on the bed beside Nancy, and they munched in silence.

A few minutes later the door opened, and Bess walked in. "Anything left for me?" she asked.

"A little," George told her. "What happened to Ted? Where did you two lovebirds go?"

Bess's blue eyes sparkled with unshed tears as she sat in the chair next to Nancy's bed. "Ted and I were saying goodbye," she said. "I'm not staying in Carmel."

Nancy wasn't entirely surprised. "What made you change your mind?" she asked, reaching out and squeezing Bess's hand.

"Ted hadn't wanted me to go look for you yesterday," Bess said. "What if we hadn't? What would have happened to you? Anyway, that got me thinking about some of the things you guys have said. I realized that every time we wanted to do something, Ted tried to stop me."

George said, "I don't want you to leave Carmel just because of what Nancy and I said. I'm sure Ted has his good side."

"But you have to admit that he hasn't shown it much since you and Nancy got here," Bess said, frowning. "I've been thinking about it a lot. There's no way I can give up all I have in River Heights for someone who's so jealous and possessive. What kind of life would that be?"

"We're sorry things didn't work out for you here," Nancy said.

"But I'm glad you're coming back home with us," George added.

Bess leaned back in her chair with a sigh. "I think I got carried away by all the compliments on my desserts," Bess admitted. "I can still bake in River Heights, and maybe I'll even get one or two good words on my desserts there."

Nancy couldn't help grinning. "Bess, you never have to ask for compliments. You *are* the greatest," she said.

She and George swooped down on Bess to wrap her in a giant hug.

Nancy's next case:

River Heights is about to elect a new mayor, and every candidate will have to take a stand on crime. But Nancy's choice, District Attorney Caroline Hill, apparently doesn't have a leg to stand on. Small-time hoodlum Bobby Rouse has implicated the DA in a bribery scandal, threatening her integrity and her chances for victory.

Nancy's convinced that Caroline is the victim of a frame-up, but before finding the proof, she has another victim on her hands—Bobby Rouse, victim of murder. Politics can be a dirty business, and it's up to Nancy to root out the corruption. Fearing that the election will be decided not by ballots but by bullets, Nancy knows this is one race she can't afford to lose . . . in *Choosing Sides,* Case #84 in The Nancy Drew Files™.

The future is in the stars . . .
the possibilities unlimited . . .
the dangers beyond belief . . .
in
the pulse-pounding new adventure

THE ALIEN FACTOR

A Hardy Boys and Tom Swift Ultra Thriller™

Tom Swift has caught a falling star—a visitor from outer space who is as beautiful as she is strange. But his secret encounter has set off alarms at the highest levels of government. To check Tom out, a top-secret intelligence agency sends two of its top operatives: Frank and Joe Hardy.

But when the alien is kidnapped, Frank and Joe and Tom realize they have to work together. They're dealing with a conspiracy that stretches from the farthest reaches of space into the deepest recesses of their own government. The fate of the country and the planet could rest on uncovering the shocking truth about the girl from another world!

COMING IN JUNE 1993